Little Bird

Little Bird

Claudia Ulloa Donoso

Translation by Lily Meyer

DEEP
VELLUM

DALLAS, TEXAS

Deep Vellum Publishing
3000 Commerce St., Dallas, Texas 75226
deepvellum.org · @deepvellum

Deep Vellum is a 501c3 nonprofit literary arts organization
founded in 2013 with the mission to bring
the world into conversation through literature.

Support for this publication has been provided in part a grant from The Dallas
Office of Arts and Culture.

ISBN: 978-1-64605-065-9 (paperback) | 978-1-64605-066-6 (ebook)

LIBRARY OF CONGRESS CONTROL NUMBER: 2021939697

Distributed by Consortium Book Sales & Distribution

Cover design by Justin Childress | justinchildress.co
Interior by KGT

Printed in the United States of America

CONTENTS

Translator's Note

Not long before releasing her convention-defying novel *Outline*, the British writer Rachel Cusk told a *Guardian* interviewer that, in the wake of critical backlash to her memoir *Aftermath*, she came to find fiction "fake and embarrassing." She continued: "Once you have suffered sufficiently, the idea of making up John and Jane and having them do things together seems utterly ridiculous." I remember reading that line and feeling both seen and sick. I write fiction in addition to translating it, and I didn't want to acknowledge the absurdity of the form to which I've devoted so much of my love and time.

Among the many beauties of Claudia Ulloa Donoso's work is that, rather than closing her eyes to the fundamental illogic of fiction, she embraces it. The stories in *Little Bird* transform the stuff of daily life — the mundane details and events that another writer might use to make an invented person seem more real—into surreal magic. She turns lawn mowing into performance art, bus rides into high drama, fly swatting into a life-or-death rescue mission. As a result, her stories feel wildly inventive even while winking constantly at the irrationality of invention. After all, the inventory of her world is exactly like the inventory of ours. How, then, does she manage to produce fiction that seems so loosely tethered to Earth?

I asked myself that question hundreds of times while translating *Little Bird*. Claudia writes in a tone like nobody else I have read. Reproducing it—or, more accurately, creating an English-language analogue to it—was a tremendous challenge, and, eventually, a mind-expanding one. Claudia's narrators approach their surroundings with a mix of innocence, bafflement, and wonder. Nearly all of them sound detached, but are, in fact, deeply emotionally invested in the story's goings-on. In order to translate them properly, I had to train myself into a version of their mental state. Rather than rejecting the confusion I sometimes felt at a character's interpretation of events, I learned to fold it into the translation process, lending my own puzzlement to the prose. Rather than deconstruct the empathy I felt and still feel for these stories' protagonists, I tried to channel it into my work.

I recognize that this sounds abstract, and potentially a little woo-woo, but translation is a vaguer art than it may seem. Substituting an English word for a Spanish one, Google can do. To my knowledge, though, no AI can yet teach itself to slip into a short story's emotional landscape, which I got used to doing every time I sat down to work on *Little Bird*. Years after first translating "Eloísa," a story in which the narrator discovers that his girlfriend's voice has magical properties, I can still readily access his precise mix of envy, insecurity, and astonished delight at having met such a woman, and I can identify those feelings in my translation choices. In my English rendition of "Eloísa," the words *I* and *my* are everywhere. Even when describing Eloísa or her surroundings, the narrator refers back to himself as much as I could make him do. His combined pride and self-doubt pop into nearly every sentence of the story. In Spanish, Claudia achieves this effect by loading sentences and passages with verbs conjugated in the first person: *volví, logré, soporté*. In English, though, the verbs for first and third person are the same—*I returned; she returned*—and multiple verbs can stack themselves behind a single pronoun. I needed a different strategy to maintain the narrator's insistent focus on himself, and so I looked for word choices and sentence structures that would force me to keep him present.

I took the opposite approach in "I Remember" and "I Don't Remember," two paired stories whose loving nostalgia, even now, makes my chest ache. Both stories seek to conjure their narrators' past selves and past lives, and so I concentrated on rendering their descriptions of the past as evocatively as I possibly could, while using very plain language for the present. My goal was to emulate Claudia's choice to tip the scales toward memory, rather than toward the sensation of remembering. Her decision here is the opposite of, to pick a famous example, Virginia Woolf's in *Mrs. Dalloway*, where Clarissa Dalloway dwells in the process of memory, variously questioning and reveling in it. Claudia's narrators just dive right in—another way, perhaps, in which she keeps her stories grounded in real and present life, but not fastened tightly to it.

Translating *Little Bird* has helped me fret less over the connection between fiction and reality, or imagination and observation. After all, the stories collected here are grounded more in personal fact than a reader might guess. Claudia wrote them after moving north of the Arctic Circle; her first summer there, she suffered severe insomnia from the endless daylight, which created the feeling of dislocation so many of her characters express. Sleep deprivation can make the everyday seem impossible or surreal—as "fake and embarrassing," to borrow Rachel Cusk's language once more, as any fiction. Reading Claudia's stories has the same effect, though far more pleasant. In her hands, surreality feels inviting, a place where I always wish to return.

I still remember the first time I entered Claudia's world. I picked *Little Bird* up in a bookstore at random, flipped through, leaned on a shelf to read the title story. When I looked up, I had that bemused, sun-dazzled feeling I associate with leaving a movie theater during the day—where am I? What time is it? How did I get here? I remember that I barely oriented myself in time to pay for the book, rather than simply taking it home. In hindsight, it seems to me that I knew, even then, that I wanted to translate the book. In actual fact, I think I just wanted to let it transport me again.

I know *Little Bird* has a similar effect on other readers. In the six years Claudia and I spent translating and revising this collection, she's won awards, been named to the Hay Festival's Bogotá 39 list of the best Latin American writers under forty, and released editions of *Pajarito*—the collection's Spanish title—in four more countries. Her fan club seems to grow every year. I feel lucky to be a member, and far luckier to have gotten to translate these stories, which I love so much. *Little Bird* taught me to appreciate fiction's absurdities, to relax my grip on reality, to read and translate with my heart before my mind. I hope it can do the same for you.

Lily Meyer
March 2021

Work Experience

Little Bird

He loves to sit and hear me sing,
Then, laughing, sports and plays with me;
Then stretches out my golden wing,
And mocks my loss of liberty.

—William Blake

I have a cat named Kokorito. He's big—fifteen pounds—and furry, and he isn't very social. His main way of showing affection is bringing me tiny dead birds. This is what cats do, I know: give their owners dead birds as presents. Or maybe trophies. Who am I to say?

Kokorito never eats the birds. He tortures them, plays with them like balls of wool, but in the end, he always leaves them in my bed, which is where I do everything these days, even eat. That's how I'm so sure the birds are for me.

My cat, who has seven lives in the Americas and nine here in Scandinavia, brings me death as a present, but the thing is, I've seen plenty of death already. I don't really need any more.

Maybe Kokorito disagrees. Maybe he thinks if I paid more attention to death, it wouldn't bother me so much. He's the expert, I guess. He has at least seven lives, like

I said, and after the twenty days he was gone last winter, he must be down a few. When he came home, he opened the window himself, drank some water, and fell asleep in my bed for two days. Then he got up, meowed, and lived again.

The birds are the best gift Kokorito has to give. Maybe he wishes he didn't have to deliver them in their death throes, beating and panting and flapping, all -ing, and then suddenly past tense. Or maybe that's the point. Maybe my cat wants me to understand that lives, except his, end in just a few seconds. Well, I get it, Kokorito. No repeats.

When I find a bird dying in my bed, I wrap it in damp paper towels, leaving its head uncovered so it can breathe. I warm the bird in my hands, clean the blood off its wings, stroke its feathers and try to open its beak. When it dies anyway, or when I find one that's already dead, I make a shroud out of Kleenex and bury it outside, or at least take the bird under the birch trees and hide it in the dry leaves.

The 2 bus from Øvre Hunstadmoen is the only one that will get me to the center of Bodø. It passes every twenty-seven minutes starting at six in the morning. I always get to my appointments early, since if I miss the bus, it's impossible not to be late.

Today, as I'm leaving for Øvre Hunstadmoen, having timed my departure perfectly in order to get downtown on schedule, I see a bird dying in the hallway, near the place where I drop my bag and take off my coat when I get home. I can't leave it there to die, but I can't miss the bus, either. I go to the kitchen, dampen a paper towel, tuck it around the bird and put it in my right coat pocket. Then I leave the house at a run.

When I get on the bus, I'm sure the driver notices that I only use my left hand. He watches me struggle to open my purse, find my wallet, pay my fare. I don't function well with one hand. He must notice, too, that my other hand is buried in my coat pocket, which means he must know that I'm hiding something. For all I know, he can tell that I'm carrying a dying bird.

Norwegians generally take off their coats as soon as they come inside because buildings in Norway are all heated. In friends' houses, they take off their shoes right away, too. Every entryway is packed with coats and jackets, so the coat stands look as bulky as men. In this office, the coats hang from the wall, looking as dead as the skinned steers at the butcher.

In an interview for a project analyst position at the Department of Culture, it's bad manners not to take off your coat when you walk into the office. It's also bad manners not to shake the interviewer's hand. If I keep my coat on, the interviewer will think I'm not open, or that I'm uncomfortable. He'll think I'm hiding something. If I don't take off my coat, he'll start to imagine what I'm hiding. He'll imagine all the way down to my underwear, and what if he doesn't imagine the right underwear for the job?

I won't be able to communicate properly if I leave my coat on. I'll sit there like an armadillo, like a turtle, like a porcupine hiding its head, showing its spines as it trundles along. All I can do to distract the interviewer from my spines is smile. When I've read tips for job interviews, they suggest that smiling helps you make a good impression. So I'll smile, but not too much. I don't want to seem nervous. My teeth are very white and once my smile won a contest at my dentist's office. My prize was twenty tubes of toothpaste, plus some fluoride.

When I smile, the interviewer smiles back. I know I should use some more body language to make a good impression, but I keep my right hand in my coat pocket even though the moment to shake hands has arrived. I have two options here: If I shake with my left hand and leave my right hand in my pocket, he'll think I'm strange, or that I'm rude for making him shake with his left when it's accepted in every country on earth that you shake hands with your right.

The other option is to remove my right hand from my pocket and offer him a damp handshake full of bird germs and, for all I know, yellow feathers, which could end up stuck to his palm. That wouldn't be a good start. But this is the option I choose. We shake hands, right to right, and it seems to go over well. I don't think he notices that my hand is a bit damp, and of course there's no way for him to know that the dampness isn't sweat but cat spit and wet paper towel and, probably, bird blood.

The interviewer talks without taking his eyes off my CV. Maybe he doesn't care that my coat is still on. He seems distracted by his own tic, if it's a tic, of opening his eyes too wide and raising his eyebrows while he talks. Still, he seems perceptive. I think he's guessed the color of my bra.

I don't want him to give me the look that the bus driver gave me this morning because I had one hand hidden in my pocket, so I hide them both. He must think that I'm shy, or nervous, but his gestures don't change. He keeps talking, opening his eyes and raising his eyebrows. I can't tell if he seems surprised or indifferent or both.

"It's very cold today," I say.

It's true. My comment is sincere, and he takes it that way, because, after I say it, he stops the interview to offer me a cup of coffee.

He comes back with two coffees and I wait for him to drink first. He slurps his coffee and then grimaces. He must have burned his tongue. Anyway, now he doesn't open his eyes quite so wide.

"I can see that you are qualified and that you're ready to take on the responsibilities associated with this position. I am sure that you would manage your projects carefully and well. We are looking for a person who will be cautious, given that the funds set aside for cultural projects have been reduced this year."

This makes me think that the job is mine, and I squeeze myself tight with excitement. Then I reach for the coffee mug in accordance with our new ritual: you take a sip; I take a sip. After that I put my hand back in my pocket, and I feel something move. The bird has come back to life.

"I only have one more question," the official says. "Why do you think that we ought to hire you?"

"Because I can take responsibility for lives other than my own."

"What does that mean?"

"Well, in terms of culture, imagine I'm in charge of organizing the Philharmonic Week. I have to be responsible for all the composers who are dead but still alive. Take Chopin. He's dead, but you and I both know that when a musician like Argerich performs his work, Chopin comes back to life and takes flight in the concert hall. Besides, when you're working on a project like the Philharmonic Week, you're in charge of the musicians in the orchestra, the singers in the choir, the conductors. Their lives are part of your job as well as their instruments."

"I understand. And could you explain how you were in charge of other people's lives at your most recent job?"

I can't explain, because now the bird is beating its wings. I can't hold it anymore. I take it from my pocket, unwrap the paper towel, and put it on top of my CV, which is still on the desk. The bird is injured. There's a spot of blood on the towel, but it's alive.

The bird gets to know me. It walks across the languages I speak fluently, then shits on my work experience. It stops on my contact information and stays still. I pick it up gently and stretch out its wings: fragile, but intact.

"It's a yellow-breasted *kjøtmeis*," I say. "When I was leaving the house to come here, I found it dying in the hallway, so I've spent this interview thinking not just about how important this job would be for my professional development and about the dead classical musicians for whom I would be responsible, to say nothing of the live musicians whom I would support, but also about saving the life of this bird. So another qualification of mine for this position is that I can stay calm and perform well under pressure."

The bird chooses this moment to fly. It circles the office, flashes like a star over the computer screens, shits again on the budget reports spooling out of the printer. It lands on the city archives and looks down at the Department of Community Administration with the proud raised head of a newly decorated veteran. The bureaucrats watch from their cubicles, spinning on their ergonomic chairs, but nobody stands. Most of them stay quiet, admiring the bird, smiling, but some are annoyed; some turn back to their screens and protect their heads and faces with sheets of printer paper.

The interviewer and I can see that it's time to open the windows.

The bird feels the cold February air rush into the office and follows it to freedom. It bounces off the photocopier and shoots out the closest window. The building is cold now, but otherwise the day has returned to normal, and I go back to the interviewer's office to finish my coffee.

When I leave the interviewer doesn't shake my hand. That doesn't concern me, since Norwegians often avoid physical contact when they say hello or goodbye. Instead, he brings back his favorite trick, opening his eyes and raising his eyebrows as he says that he'll call me. I believe him and smile to show it.

On the way home I see plenty of birds, but I'm looking for the one that kept me company during the interview. I'd like to say thank you. Sometimes it's a good idea to carry dying animals around, to keep your hands in your pockets, and to never take off your coat.

Puppeteer

When I was sixteen, I decided I was born to be a puppeteer, but life has taken me in another direction. I work at a hotel desk, and sometimes I feel like a puppet. My boss, the manager, the HR head, and the guests hold the strings, and there I am, smiling away, speaking in a voice far too polite to be real.

But no more. Today, at twenty-six, I'm setting out on my true path.

I start with the puppet I've made of my boss. I lift his arms and imitate his bird's voice. "The receptionist is the smartest employee this hotel has. She should be in charge. She's very pretty, too. I just wish she knew it."

I do the same with the head of HR, speaking in his bored lion's growl. "Yes, she's very talented. We're going to promote her for sure. Did you know she speaks five languages? You know, we really should consider her petition to change the uniform."

Now I move the general manager, raising his arms and giving him a nice tenor voice. "I'm a terrible puppeteer. I'm a failure. I don't let my puppets stay in character. This receptionist isn't even a receptionist. She's a princess from a different play. I should never have put her in this shitty Holiday Inn."

This is how my first performance ends. I've moved my marionettes, held their hands up while I do their voices. The pistol in my hand isn't quite the same as the cords that move most puppets' limbs, but in the end, it works just as well.

Wood

Every so often, they ask me to work a few shifts at the sawmill. There's nothing hard about it, though you do risk losing a hand. But I worked for years in a master carpenter's shop, so I know how to saw wood in straight lines.

Work at the mill never changes. You cut wood into long rectangles or matching squares. My technique is to spread my palms on a board and push it into the saw's mouth. I arch my back like a cat waking up, then stretch my whole body toward the blade. I'm comfortable; I'm not frightened. It's like I'm still half asleep.

While I cut wood yesterday, I thought about writing. I've discovered that danger combined with boredom creates the ideal situation for me to write. I used to think I needed silence and solitude, but lately that's all I've had, and it turns out not to work. I haven't written at all. I just fill the silence and solitude with movies and the sounds of my household appliances.

I thought it was my job at the vet's that stopped me from writing. There were days I licked my asshole and mewed after lunch. I opened my wings like a bird when I was running to catch the bus or barked when strangers came near me.

Yesterday in the sawmill, words fell as fast as wood shavings. I wrote a whole story in my head. When I got home, though, I was exhausted. I lay down on the sofa and fell asleep with my whole body still smelling of pine.

I forgot the story.

I dreamed that I was a pine tree. When pines are faced with wind strong enough to break them, they produce a new layer of wood, distinct from the rest of the trunk. We get hurricane winds from the south here, and so our pine trees are covered in this wood, which helps them stay upright. But it's not armor against the wind. Instead, it makes the pines flexible. They duck from the storm's gaze, and no matter how furiously the wind blows, the pines blow with it. They stay calm.

Only the trees know their own strength. Each one understands the rest. They sway in the wind, each tree watching the one ahead, until the wind dissipates among their branches, defeated, its howls as hopeless as a preacher warning sleeping lions that the End of Days is near.

*

A stereogram is an optical illusion.

This illusion comes from the eye's ability to capture images from more than one angle. The brain combines the two images, so when you look at a stereogram you see one image in 3D.

You make a stereogram by superimposing two photographs taken from slightly different perspectives.

It won't work unless the viewer knows beforehand that when she blurs her eyes, she'll see in 3D.

I have superimposed a photograph from my childhood and one from the year I was twenty-six: me sitting on the same sofa in my parents' house, the same expression on my face, same almost-smile that doesn't quite make it, same hair in the same style, same posture, same crossed legs and same hands in my lap.

I blur my eyes and now I see myself in 3D, sitting on the sofa, getting older.

Now the passage of time doesn't bother me so much.

See, I've proved that aging is only an illusion. Aging is what happens when we confuse our brains by putting too many images together at once. We think we see a picture, but the truth is, we're just staring into space.

Developments

I found a part-time job in a photography studio.

It's easy, just sitting at a computer. My job is to develop pictures, but all that means is hitting print. I like the work because I'm a bit of a voyeur. I love looking at photos of strangers. It's very entertaining.

Today I looked at forty-five pictures of a girl's birthday party.

It was her twenty-fifth. I saw the candles on her cake, I saw all her presents, I saw her friends and family, I saw her sober and drunk. I saw her face when she wasn't looking at the camera and when she was forcing a smile. I saw who she loved the most at the party and who she didn't care about that much, and I saw that she was happy for some of the party, but she was overwhelmed sometimes, too, and sometimes she wanted it to end.

Today I've also seen a wedding, a fishing trip, a

birthday party for a cute little kid. I saw a family dinner—they had to be related, they all had the same face—and a funeral.

I stopped my work to study the funeral. I wanted to know who was grieving and who was pretending. Then I made a list. I took notes about all of them, and then I gave them names and relationships to the dead man.

The whole project was difficult because in funeral photos pretty much no one smiles. I say *pretty much* because smiling for the camera is a reflex. We learn how to do it as children. Anyway, that's how I spent the afternoon, taking notes, studying the funeral pictures in depth while I printed out other photos.

I'd always suspected I could figure out a lot with the studio computer, so I focused on the details, read the messages on the floral wreaths, tried to connect the names on the wreaths to the people in the photos. Now I know the dead man's name, and his relatives'. I figured out his age. I know what cemetery he's in because I saw some pictures of the burial, too.

It made me really sad. It's always upsetting when you know the story of someone who's died.

This afternoon a woman came to pick up the funeral photos. I'm supposed to act like I never saw the pictures—studio rules—but I got up enough courage to say, "I'm sorry if I'm overstepping, but I wanted to offer my condolences."

I gave her a quick hug, then asked if she wanted any of the photographs enlarged.

She didn't want any enlargements, of course. When I told her I was sorry, she made a gesture of thanks. That was when I looked in her eyes and saw what I'd guessed from the photos: she was happy that her husband had died.

I guess the pictures must be for her kids, or else they'll end up in some attic full of junk.

Before she left the studio, she said, "Actually, I do want a picture blown up. This one."

In the picture she's standing with her kids, and behind her a man who's not part of the family is taking her hand. You can barely see him in the photo, but I know he's there because the development program we use lets you sketch in the rest of a body when only a little bit appears in the photograph.

He must be her lover.

I almost told her she had no shame, no respect for her newly dead husband, why didn't she blow up a picture of herself with the dead man, or her kids, or the one of the funeral chapel with all the candles burning. I almost asked her who blows up a funeral photo, what is she, crazy?

But I shut up and wrote down the order. I did it for professional reasons, because it's not good to lose clients, especially not ones like this woman. I'm curious. I can't wait to see the first photos of her on vacation with her new man.

A Writer's Pastimes

I've decided to stop writing. My books are in every bookstore in the country, but I live alone and I drink too much. I eat out of cans, and I smoke more than ever. Some people might find this bohemian. They might think it helps me pick up women, or sell books, but the truth is, I'm a sad son of a bitch. All I want is to go back to my old ways. I want to do the things I did before I started to write. Collect screws, for example.

In my collection I have more than three hundred screws of different materials, including plastic. The screws are grouped and classified by the date and location where I found them. I don't just buy them in hardware stores. No, these screws are special, like people. That's how I feel about them. Alone in the street, the screws are like runaways. They've escaped from a life stuck in place, one of many, supporting someone else's weight. Maybe they'll rust outside, but better to rust to death than sit motionless in an old man's replacement hip or clack around in an old woman's dentures, listening to her gripe about the pigeons that nest on her balcony. I have that type of screw, you know. I find them near hospitals. They're one of my most important groups.

I got my favorite screw at a burial. The lid of the coffin hadn't been securely attached, and as the coffin descended into the grave it fell open to reveal the dead man's face. The cemetery workers didn't stop shoveling. The mourners didn't stop watching. No one spoke. We stood there in black, not moving, not crying, as the dry earth fell on the dead man's face. It looked like cocoa on top of a cake at first, but before long they had covered him completely. I was sure the escaped screw was waiting for me somewhere, and when I looked, there it was: a silver screw with the funeral home's initials, which, incidentally, are the same as mine.

I walked for more than four hours and didn't find a single screw. At home, the consequences of my literary success are there to greet me. The cat is sleeping on the warm top of the television I never turn off. Something smells rotten. A light on the answering machine blinks red. Two messages, the first is a woman sighing, which effectively conveys irritation without speech: a message from her. The second is me saying, "Buy cat food and dandruff shampoo." I used to hate hearing my own voice. Now it happens every day.

I got a letter from her today, too. She was angry when she wrote it. I can tell because she pressed down so hard with the pen that I can almost read her words like Braille. She says I have to stop writing to her, but I've never written her a letter. What I do, and have done for a while, is send her clippings of my reviews and interviews, articles I've written, signed book covers and so on. No special dedication, of course. I send her everything that has my name or picture on it. This way it will be hard for her to forget me.

I wonder what bothers her so much about getting mail from me. Maybe it's the smell of tobacco, which seeps into whatever I touch. It's probably invaded her house. I bet it leaves a fog that hurts her eyes when she tries to sew, sends her housekeeper into fits, makes her fat husband sweat and turn red. She must have to look at him for a long time to prove that she's concerned, and then kiss his slick bald spot, even though what she feels, deep down, is disgust and loneliness, which I know because those are the emotions her letter evokes in the reader.

Or maybe my signature annoys her. It's chaotic, illegible. Maybe it reminds her of me. Anyway, it doesn't matter now that I'm not going to be a writer anymore. I'll have to stop bothering her, because pretty soon I'm going to run out of clippings to send.

I light a cigarette and her image disappears with the first mouthful of warm, bitter smoke, a white snake that slides down my throat in order to nest in my lungs. The cat trains his green eyes on me. He's angry because the scrape of my lighter, which always takes a few tries to work, woke him up. He stretches until his hair bristles with static and he looks like a stuffed animal. Then he licks his paws and goes back to his dreams, where I'm sure he's an enormous cat, hunting elephants.

Yesterday in a bar I tried a liquor called Partner and liked it. I ordered ten shots and poured them into an empty half-liter bottle of Concordia soda that I had in the pocket of my coat. Today I looked for Partner in the grocery store and a few liquor stores, but I didn't find it. When I drink from the plastic bottle, though, it tastes the same, even though it's been sitting in there all night, maybe mixing with the last few drops of soda.

After the bar I went to a new bookstore called Neon, named after the lights in the shelves. I don't think neon works in a bookstore. For me, neon belongs in the greasy spoons where I've gotten salmonella more than once; the casinos where I've lost everything, even my watch; and those trendy brothels that look like restaurants or discos or hostels till you go inside.

I spent an hour looking around the bookstore, studying the effect of neon light on my skin. Then I started to look at other writers' jacket photos, both famous authors and relative unknowns. Some, like me, looked good under the fluorescents. Others turned the color of death. I found a pocket edition of one of my books and noticed that in the jacket photo I looked younger and cleaner. Retouched, for sure.

I liked the photo and decided to send it to her, since she might not have it yet. When I was ready to leave, I found the book and put it in my coat. I'm not sure why. I could afford to buy it, of course.

I didn't expect an alarm to go off when I left. Most of the bookstores I go to are secondhand ones, the kind with energy-saving light bulbs, stores where even the booksellers smell stale. A security system wouldn't be worth the bother in that kind of store. It would be like trying to catalogue dust or put a safety seal on the distant past.

I felt my cheeks turning red, but I stayed calm and kept walking as if nothing was wrong. Outside the guard stopped me and, seeming embarrassed, told me he had to pat me down. First he found the bottle, then the book. He was short and fat, this guard, with a wide smile and crooked teeth, and he recognized my face on the book cover. He shook my hand and asked me to sign a book. Not the one I'd stolen, but one he had in his pocket already, in which the protagonist is a highly respected bank guard, successful with women, powerful and immortal with his revolver and bulletproof vest.

The guard let me leave with the book. I saw him go inside the store and tell the cashier something; she smiled and waved me away. I smiled back and wiped the guard's sweat off my palm.

I left.

As I walked, I saw the guard return to his post, stroking his revolver with satisfaction. He winked at the cashier, but she just kept painting her nails and blowing bubbles of pink gum.

The cat scratched my face while I slept. Now he's hiding behind a stack of newspapers and it's too late for revenge. All I can do is swear at him. I'm a bit drunk, and I only have one cigarette left. I finish the Partner in my Concordia bottle, cut my photograph out of the book I stole yesterday, and sift through my papers for some cardstock to put on the back. I find a good piece: neon blue. When I turn the photo over to glue it down, there's the anti-theft chip. I imagine her putting me in her wallet, then walking into Neon to buy a book and setting off the alarm. Maybe she'll be with her husband when it happens. The guard will stop her, and she'll have to show him my retouched photo on the neon blue background. I'll look great. The guard will be a hero for exposing her treachery; her husband will be a cuckolded idiot; she'll be a wily cheater; the cashier will be a mosquito buzzing in her ear, making everything worse; and I'll be there too, handsome on neon blue cardstock, surrounded by cheap little characters shouting on and on, the alarm in the background shrilling a warning forever.

The envelope is waiting, already stamped. Before I cover the security chip with glue, I study it. Just a sticker, really. When I turn it from side to side it glints like metal, or like the holographic comic-book cards you got in candy bars when I was young.

I look at the chip till I feel the same impatience and despair that I felt trying to find my heroes in those cards. Maybe this one has the name of the bookstore, or a factory employee's face. Or maybe the face inside is mine.

First Person

Today in class we went over the regular verb *vivir*.

The Spanish 1—5:30–7:00—Beginners conjugated the verb perfectly in the first-person singular present.

Vivo.

And they said: I live in a red house, I live at Kongengsgate 23, I live in Bodø.

I wrote their examples on the board: two lines V, one line I, two lines V, one circle O.

VIVO.

I wrote *vivo* eleven times in white chalk. By the end I was exhausted, and I had a knot in my throat.

The problem is that now I have to tell my class, so pleased with themselves for understanding *vivir*, that *vivir* doesn't only mean moving into a house, having an address, picking a city or country where you belong.

I read *vivo* eleven times and thought about my many lives, like a cat's. I watched them pass until I reached today, saw myself living and living and living all over again.

My voice broke as I told my eleven students, "You know, *vivir* has another meaning too, but it's not worth learning right now."

Right now, I can't explain.

That kind of *vivir*, the book says, is Advanced.

Lifeguard

Today I went to campus to register for next semester. It's my last year and all I have left are electives. When I got to the window, I told the man in charge of registration I needed help. I didn't know what classes to take.

"Let me pull up your transcript."

He clicked until he'd found my history. Then he suggested Political Science, International Politics, Globalization, and Arctic Civilizations.

"Arctic Civilizations sounds good. I'm into polar bears."

"What else are you into?"

"I don't know."

"You don't know what you like?"

"I like polar bears and your purple shirt. Maybe history. I could try some history."

While he searched for history courses, a fly appeared. It buzzed around his head, landed on his sleeve, and started to walk. The man was still searching. He was unstoppable. He moved his hand on the mouse and kept his eyes on the screen. I watched the fly climb his shirt, explore his chest, traverse his arms and neck, set out for the pink skin of his ears. It was like the bug didn't know it could fly. Maybe it wanted to walk.

As I watched the bug traverse the man's head, its body huge and dark in his fine blond hair, I began to think I was looking at a dead man.

If I found a dead man on the street, the first thing I would do would be to search his pockets for ID.

I would find his name.

It was engraved in black letters on a silver nametag. Bjørn.

"Bjørn, you're dying," I said.

The bug took flight.

He raised his head and looked directly at me. The silence filled my stomach like food. I don't know how to describe his expression, but I was afraid. Maybe it wasn't fear. Maybe it was a combination of rage and blue sadness, blue like the color of his eyes.

"Here are your classes, María."

He'd called me by name; I'd called him by name. It was all so strange and dense. It felt like we were at a trial and the judge was about to deliver the ruling.

He handed me my registration sheet, but before I left his office, I looked for the fly. I looked everywhere, on top of each object, in every shadow and corner, but the fly had disappeared.

I felt seasick. I couldn't find the bug. Nausea hit me like a wave. The room was too bright, then too dark. I had goose bumps and chills. I managed to keep walking even though my sight had fogged up and I felt like ants were marching over my skin, but somehow I got myself to the cafeteria and asked for a bottle of water.

The girl who rang me up had a fly walking across her forehead. I swatted it right away, flicking my registration at her face, barely missing her eyes. She smiled, surprised. "We get bugs sometimes. I think it happens when they cook fish."

I didn't answer. I moved toward the tables and felt the weight of my body, the thick blood moving in my limbs, the air in my lungs, my legs as I took each slow step, like a lifeguard emerging from the water, dragging a big, heavy body like Bjørn's.

But remember, I saved that girl's life.

*

"You look sad."

"Just preoccupied."

"Why?"

"I fucked up at work. I think I'm going to get fired."

". . ."

"Imagine you're a theater tech. You're in charge of the curtain, the rugs, that kind of thing. One day you're carrying a rolled-up red carpet, very heavy, the one from opening night, and you're up on a catwalk and the carpet slips out of your hands and falls on a row of theatergoers, breaking their necks, *crack, crack,* as it unrolls, until it's covered half the audience and an actress—the villain in the show, and a bad actress, too— thinks it's a new part of the staging and in the middle of her monologue steps triumphantly onto the red carpet, and everybody leaves the theater and it's just the bad actress, the broken necks, and you."

"Since when do you work in a theater?"

"Oh, I don't. I'm a waitress. And today I was pouring a very expensive red wine and the bottle slipped out of my hand. The glass I was filling broke, *crack.* The wine looked like a red carpet on the tablecloth, and the whole table of guests gave me these tragic faces, like bad actors."

"I don't think you're in the right job."

Between Us

A Bollywood Story

This morning, a young man with a thick accent stopped me on the street. In an urgent, bewildered voice, he asked whether I was Hindu.

"I am," I told him right away, speaking Spanish. *Sí soy.*

The man moved away from me. He sat down on a street bench and burst into tears. He talked while he wept, but I had no idea what he was saying. He looked at me like he wanted to be comforted. He kept shaking his head and clutching his chest.

Once, I saw a documentary about Indians who walk on coals in order to cleanse their souls. I could tell this man's soul was pretty tangled. I wondered whether he had burn scars on the bottom of his feet.

I sat down on the bench without speaking, then took a package of Kleenex from my purse and pressed it into his hands. Then I tried to signal that I was listening by raising my eyebrows and arranging my mouth into a gentle smile.

He dried his face with a Kleenex, then started speaking. His language was musical and unfamiliar, like the first time I heard a song in Persian. I couldn't understand a word, but it was beautiful.

While he told me his life story, I studied his gestures. He had dry skin and a way of moving between expressions so fast he seemed surprised, angry, confused, and desolate all at once. Periodically he smiled sarcastically—more of a grimace than a smile—and patted the air, like he was bouncing a basketball.

I listened, repeating, "Sí soy," every so often. He'd reacted so strongly to the first one that I assumed it had to be meaningful in Hindi. For all I knew, it was a religious mantra: *sisoyyyyy*.

When I wasn't talking, I kept my head cocked to the side, though I worried it made me look like a dog trying to understand a human. Every so often, I moved my hand the way he did, as if dribbling another invisible basketball, and smiled. Other times, I swept my hands to the sides like I was clearing a table or turned my head in disapproval. I wanted him to know I was listening, that I empathized, and that I wanted to help.

He behaved as if I understood him completely.

Suddenly he lowered his brows and crossed his arms, telegraphing: That's it. I smiled widely, glad that the drama—whatever it was—had reached its conclusion.

That was, in fact, it.

"Patni pati," he said, smiling.

I didn't want him to stop smiling, and so I nodded. "Patni pati sí soy."

Then he reached into his pocket and produced a diamond in a gold setting. He put it on my right ring finger, then wrapped my small hand in his big, rough palms. His hands covered mine completely. I couldn't even see the ring, but I was happy to accept it. He hugged me hard, then touched my face, the way Bollywood heroes do before kissing the heroines.

I checked my watch, which said I needed to head home. I got up and prepared for my exit, like a princess at the end of a play. When I began walking, he didn't stop me. Instead, he came along.

Now I'm home with a Hindu stranger on my sofa, and we're engaged.

I need to make my fiancé dinner, but the only appropriate food I have to offer is instant tikka masala from a packet. I know from documentaries that Indian marriages involve a red circle on the bride's forehead, so I give myself one with ketchup, then ask, "Tikka masala?"

He smiles and hugs me, so he must like the circle.

I can put incense on the table, and yellow flowers. I have an Indian-print skirt in my closet, plus a bag, a scarf, and a pair of sandals that say *Made in India*.

I can tell he's starting to relax. He took off his shoes,

37

at least, so soon I'll be able to check for burn scar on his feet. He must have them. I'm sure he has a clean soul.

All my books were right. Fate gives you signs, and today I had the light to see. I have escaped my bad karma and my solitude. I have been reborn, and so far, it's been perfect. As the prophet says: The Universe has conspired to grant my wish.

Now, all I have to do is take the Sacred Heart off the wall and hang a portrait of Shiva instead. I don't want to start a serious relationship on the wrong foot.

Line

The first thing I saw when I came home today was a stranger at my kitchen table.

"The door was open, so I came in," I told him as I felt for my Swiss Army knife in my pocket.

It wasn't there.

I was scared, so I smiled.

He smiled back.

While I took off my coat I thought about my knife: did the stranger have it, how would it feel to stick a knife in someone's body, would there be blood, would there be a yellow liquid instead if I stabbed him in the liver.

I sat at the table with him and he asked if I wanted coffee.

He made it carefully, attentively. He found the coffee beans, read the labels, and asked if I wanted black coffee or a cappuccino. Then he opened the bags and smelled them, considered for a few seconds, and picked the grounds in the red bag, which I would have done, too. He washed out the espresso pot before he filled it, heated milk in a pan and whisked it gently till it foamed.

He handed me the cinnamon from the spice rack and sat at the table in my usual seat. I drank my cappuccino slowly, looked around from the chair I never sat in. My whole house looked new.

"You don't want anything?"

"No, I had breakfast already," he said. There were breadcrumbs on the counter, and the butter was still out of the fridge, next to a cup—the ugly one with the clowns, which I never touch—with orange pulp stuck to its sides.

While he drank water, I finished my perfect cappuccino and studied my house from the guest's seat. Maybe the room just looked better from that angle. Maybe that's why I always put my guests there. I don't remember how I picked my spot. When you move into a house you choose a seat at the table, a side of the bed, a spot in the shower. You don't know why you choose. It just happens. For all I know, we unconsciously pick the worst spots in the house so that we can impress guests when they come. All we care about is appearances, even at home. What bullshit.

"You have a nice house," I told him.

"Thanks." He smiled. "Honestly, I didn't decorate it myself."

For a moment I thought he was going to take a

kitchen knife and stab me, saying, The house was yours, but it's mine now. I'd bleed to death and it would be like a scene from some second-rate horror movie.

Instead of the horror movie, he poured me more coffee and asked, "How was your day?" so I told him where I'd gone, what I'd done, the mess I'd made at work, how I was pretty sure I was going to get fired.

"Well, sometimes when one door closes, another opens," he said. Then he finished his water and burped, but he covered his mouth and said excuse me.

He cleared the table and looked at the clock, then started making dinner. I sat by the window and fiddled with the box where I keep silverware, opening and closing the lid. My Swiss Army knife was in there. He was frying a steak, and when he shut his eyes because the grease was spitting, I smuggled the knife into my pocket.

While he cooked, he told me he was a writer. He had a book coming out soon, called *White Lines*.

"Coke?"

He laughed, and I felt stupid. "Everyone writes about cocaine," he said. "Not me."

He explained that he got his title from the highway. He'd spent a long time on the road, first as a long-distance trucker, then as a hitchhiker. One day he decided to measure all the white lines he saw, and he found that they were exactly the same everywhere he went.

"Even out of the country they're the same. Think about it: a worker in China paints the same line, in the same way, maybe at the same time as a worker here, painting lines on the highway that gets you to the jungle."

In the book, he measured in highway lines instead of kilometers. He'd made an inventory of lines and grouped them by time and place. Each group went with a story, with photographs and postcards, and with calculations and diagrams that demonstrated the relationship between the lines and the writer's life.

I was so interested in the book that I got interested in him, too. We talked about our lives for the whole meal. We opened a bottle of wine, then another. By the end of the night, we were drunk. We danced in the living room and wound up naked on the carpet, making love.

When I took my clothes off, my Swiss Army knife fell to the ground. He picked it up, opened it, and ran the blade over my skin so lightly I could have died of pleasure.

The next morning, I woke up late. I ran out of the house, but still didn't get to work on time. They fired me and I didn't care.

I got home and he wasn't there. He'd left me a note: "Treat this house like your own."

I got in the shower and saw the line he'd left on my body. The skin wasn't broken, just red. The scratch started at my throat and went all the way down to the place where my legs separated. It made me picture myself on an operating table, split open like a corpse during an autopsy. I thought about science-class frogs, the chicken I was going to cook later, that line where if you did open me up, you'd see my beating heart, my working guts. As I dried off, I thought about highways.

I've measured the line on my body, and now I'm measuring lines on the highway. There are lots of trucks rushing angrily by; they honk at me, stop short, the truckers staring while I hike my shirt up and stretch myself on the ground, still holding my measuring tape, which writhes like a snake in the wind.

The Wrong Girl

yesterday / all of us piled on the ground / like drunk
sheep at that party / I decided, tonight I won't speak
    yesterday
    I just wanted to listen to you
    you were talking about the ipod / about liverpool
and rosemborg / about wireless internet and ip calling
you were talking about svein's ex / about oasis / about
oslo / about your dead cat / you talked about snow /
your new shoes / the different types of gold / about turkey / pork / putting mayonnaise on lobsters / you said
you hate lettuce / also anchovies / capers / you started
to use the word versus / coming down hard on the *u*
/ like you'd studied latin at some seminary in the 20s
/ glenfiddich vs the famous grouse / liverpool vs man-
chester / coke vs hash / red vs white / belle and sebastian vs I forget what band

you talked a lot about belle and sebastian / enthu-
siastically / happily / like they were your neighbors

belle and sebastian eating at your table / using your
bathroom / drinking your wine / as if you saw them
every day / when they take out the trash / or walk the
dog

I had a glass in my hand / my fifth rum and fanta /
my face was red / my jacket was red / all my senses were
fogged

and then you asked me / or someone asked me /
what do you think of belle and sebastian?

they're the kind of band that makes music inspired
by the dentist, think about it, the drill in your molar
going *dear catastrophe waitress*... but no, really they're
influenced by the supermarket, it's music to push a
cart to, music for filling your basket with canned beans
and lettuce and potatoes ... belle and sebastian pushing a cart, making a list: toilet paper, boxed wine, clo-
rox, bread, napkins, fish, coffee, jam... and then when
they pay they smile real big at the checkout girl who
hums their song all day like a mantra: *step into my office
baby*.

that's what I said / mostly to fuck with you

I guess it was blasphemy / at that party where
everyone was named / either belle / or sebastian

my name's claudia / no one was talking about me
/ not even you

so around 3 a.m. / when I saw the full moon / and my eyes were all rum / and all I heard was

belle and sebastian

belle and sebastian

belle and sebastian

like a broken record

I looked out the window / and saw the moon / was stained

I stood up / got my coat / washed my hands / called a taxi

I left

without making noise / so no one would notice

in the taxi / I told the driver / I was the first person to leave that party / and it's not even late / and the driver said / now they're talking about you

I leaned on the door / smiled at the driver / looked at the moon / and felt better.

Plant

Sometimes, when you move in with somebody—*with somebody*, I mean, not a cousin or friend, not your brother, not your mother; when you move in with your partner, sometimes the first thing you buy for your new house is a plant.

I thought we'd gotten an anthurium (*Anthurium*), but it turns out that I have a peace lily, or *fredslilje* (*Spathiphyllum*). At least they belong to the same family: *Araceae*. I learned this recently, when a man with thick glasses installed himself in my living room and—for a reason that remains unclear to me—began staring at my plant.

I wanted to tell him the story of my plant, that it was little when I bought it, that I paid 75KR for it but then I paid 200KR for a bigger pot so it could grow. I wanted to tell him that when you move in with your boyfriend, you buy plants. It's not hard to figure out: first you take care of a plant, but later there will be more plants, or cats, or children, to fill the rooms of your house.

(The pot looks like a head, don't you think?)

But all I said about my plant was that it was an anthurium and it was the first plant I'd owned in this country. The man with the glasses, who was an educated, cultured individual, informed me that it was a peace lily, not an anthurium. He wouldn't stop looking at it. The thing is, the peace lily wasn't doing too well. I was embarrassed, watching him look at it. It was like I had an infected cut, and he was staring at my scabbed, oozing skin.

The truth is, the relationship I have with my plant now that I live alone is a lot like my relationship with myself. Before, there were three of us here. There was someone else to pay attention to whether the plant's leaves were drying up, whether it needed direct sun or fresh air. That was a while ago. Now it's just me and my plant. When its leaves get withered, I worry, but I know it won't die. Every time I see that it's suffering, I go straight to the kitchen, fill the measuring cup with cold water, and give it a liter to drink in one gulp.

After he'd gotten his fill of the plant, the man started looking at me. He stared into my eyes without blinking, like we were kids having a staring contest, and whoever blinks first loses and is weak. This time, no one blinked, but it wasn't a contest. While he looked at me, he ran his hand over my hair and along my neck and rested it on the back of my head. I let him touch me. I swallowed spit and let him feel me swallow. When he moved his hand again, he put it under my chin, pressing his fingers into the soft spots. He squeezed my mouth open like he was prying the lid off an Ikea box, my jaw approaching his, a box falling open to show not furniture, but teeth and a tongue hidden inside.

After the kiss I got up from the sofa and the man went back to studying my plant. I kept wanting to tell him what I thought about couples buying plants together, and the pot looking like a head, and how the plant must be a male plant because it had never flowered. I was afraid he'd misinterpret my ideas, though, and think I was inviting him to move in. I was also afraid that he'd correct me about male plants and tell me that all plants are hermaphrodites, or at least bisexuals, so I didn't talk about my plant anymore. I don't know very much about plants, or anything else. After we'd been there a while, me standing and the man sitting, it occurred to me to take a picture of the plant before we all had a drink.

I went to the kitchen and brought in the measuring cup full of cold water in one hand, a bottle of cava and two glasses in the other. I watered the plant while the man poured the wine. When I went back to the sofa, we started the staring contest again, but this time my eyes turned red and started to water, which had nothing to do with the contest and is not proof that I'm weak. It was because I could hear the plant drinking water, and

I knew it had been thirsty for a long time, and now it was trying to get itself together so it could keep on living with me.

(Which must be hard, I know.)

While the plant soaked up the last of its water the man with glasses and I drank our cava too quickly so it felt like we were drowning in bubbles, so it stung our throats, so it hit our stomachs in white, foaming cascades.

We were both thirsty, I guess. Or dying.

The man's come back several times now. He sits on my sofa, but my plant's doing better, so he doesn't stare at it anymore. What bothers me is that every time, before we start the staring and kissing, he's staring at something else that knows me well, some other object that's lived with me for a long time.

Eloísa

Before Eloísa, I was lonely and insecure, and at the start of our relationship it was hard for me to accept the men in her life. Now, I understand how good the situation is for us both.

Eloísa and I met online. After we exchanged messages for a while, she suggested that we meet in person, and she seduced me with her compliments, her silver tongue. What a quiet man like me needs, it turns out, is a woman who can talk.

Eloísa quickly got into the habit of staying at my house. At first she just slept over, but before long her visits were so frequent it was as if we were living together. Our daily routines strengthened my confidence that she would stay. Slowly I believed in her enough to observe her, and then I noticed her moving my things.

I first saw it happen at dinner. Before we ate, she shuffled the cups and silverware around the table as if she were setting up a Ouija board. A few days later I noticed her doing the same with books, with lamps, all the objects that build up around a house. It made me nervous. I knew from experience that women acquire odd habits when they start to cheat. I got uncomfortable in her presence and began to worry about how little I knew of her life. For instance, I'd never seen her house. She always had some reason why it was better for me not to come over, and I accepted her excuses in order to be polite. I did know her address, which meant I knew she lived in a poor neighborhood far away, but no matter how much I wondered and suffered, I wasn't brave enough to ask her to tell me more.

One day, finally, I just went. She lived at the edge of the neighborhood, in one of the few residential buildings left on a street full of fast-food restaurants. The air was full of fog and a grease so thick it hid the beggars and prostitutes and stray dogs as they went about their days. Outside her building I buzzed an apartment at random and a child's voice came through the intercom. I asked him nicely to let me in, and he agreed.

I walked down the hall and found that it ended in a bright courtyard with a pond surrounded by thick conifers, pomegranate bushes, and terra-cotta pots full of flowers. The garden seemed as exotic as Eloisa herself. Maybe I'm wrong not to trust her, I told myself. Maybe she's just different, but before I could convince myself further, I was interrupted by an old woman who appeared in the patio and demanded, "What do you want? What are you doing here?"

"I'm sorry. I'm just looking for Eloísa."

"So why didn't you buzz her?"

"I don't know her apartment number."

"Well, she's not around, so be a nice boy and get out. We're all sick of having her strange men here."

I went home. I managed to spend the night next to Eloísa without showing how unsettled I was. The next day, we got ready for work together, but the second she was dressed, I dragged her into the garage. She cried, but I didn't let it get to me. I grabbed her arm and pushed her into the car. For a long time, we drove in silence, but as we approached her neighborhood, she at last began to talk.

Eloísa's apartment was the biggest dump I'd ever seen. It was a mess. In a few corners you could see that someone might have tried to organize, but in the way an insane person would: there were clothes in the refrigerator, pots on the sofa, crockery everywhere, canned food piled next to the bathtub. The thought of her living in this mess overwhelmed me with emotion. I couldn't tell if I was furious or ashamed until a man appeared from her bedroom.

Eloísa said, almost whispering, "Please don't hurt him. I already explained this to you. I'll open the door and he'll leave."

He went, all right, but his attitude, like he didn't care in the slightest, disturbed me even more. My legs gave out beneath me, and Eloísa knelt at my side. Then she started to clear the apartment's junk away, and I saw that what she'd told me was true.

The plague of fireflies began several years ago. She didn't want to call the exterminator. Instead, she turned the building's communal patio into a garden, thinking the insects would rather light up in nature than in her room. But even when the garden was in bloom the bugs didn't leave, and this is what happened next: she started to talk to them, and, as if they couldn't resist her words any more than I could, the fireflies turned into men.

She tried to get to know these people she'd created, but though the firefly-men could speak, they couldn't have a conversation. If they talked too much, they fell apart. Their bodies withered on her floor and then rotted. She mourned them every time. She turned into a recluse for a while, locked herself in her apartment to figure out how to get rid of the fireflies, but all she could do was wave the bugs toward the open windows and hope that they'd fly away.

Living in silence, unable to come and go as she wanted, was torture. There were times when she got fed up with her own kindness and tore the house apart, which just made the situation worse. She'd go into hysterics, and her shrieking filled the house with men.

Most left when she opened the door, but some stayed. She had to talk to them till they disintegrated. It was a vicious cycle. The insects heard her talking to the men and as the men fell apart, the insects began to transform.

Eloísa decided she'd never speak to a man in person again. Then she met me. Staying at my house makes it easier for her to talk the remaining firefly-men to death when she goes home. She feeds their remains to the street dogs. Every so often we go to her apartment together and she tries to get me to talk to the fireflies. She's convinced that if I try hard enough, I can make a woman. I'm nice to them, but all I can do is get a few bugs to turn into gelatinous heaps that, if you squint, bear some resemblance to the female form.

The truth is, I don't want to talk to other women. I only go along because I know she wants to feel chosen; she wants to feel special. That's how women are: if they want to shine, it's less to trap men than to make other women go dark.

Eloísa likes to claim that she talks to the fireflies in order to make me new friends, but I know that's not true. I know her eloquence is just a cover for her insecurity. She'll never say it out loud, but I know she needs to compare me to other men to know she's made a good choice.

After she makes men out of fireflies, she leaves me alone with them. I open beers and we drink together in silence before I let them out the door. Together, we don't need to prove ourselves. We know that, no matter how dim and intermittent our light, we are complete beings. We are free.

Between Us

"Would you please close the door?"

I closed it, and for a moment we remained in darkness. Then he turned on the light, and I saw him sitting on his side of the closet with his Discman, surrounded by his gorgeous dress shirts. I sat on my side with a book in my lap, all my dresses and perfumes around me.

One Sunday, months ago, he looked at me over breakfast and said, "It's got to be the closet. The most private place in the house. In there, the only thing between us is the mirror, and even that shows our true selves."

Now we spend our afternoons in the closet. When I told Silvia, she said we were crazy. At that point, I was already convinced Víctor was losing his mind, but he insisted. He said the closet was a form of therapy. We rarely talked in there, but still, he said, sitting in such a small space brought us closer.

"Honestly, Silvia, we're not doing too well."

"And you think you can turn it around in the closet?"

"Who knows."

I kissed Silvia goodbye, paid for her coffee, and went home to find Víctor reading the paper and jiggling his left leg uncontrollably, like he did the day he proposed. It made me nervous, but I kissed him and said, "I had coffee with Silvia. She says hello. She might come over next week."

Víctor put his glasses in their case, then rolled up the newspaper. "Would you do me a favor?" he said. "I'd like you to sleep in the guest room from now on, and I'd like you to start tonight."

I was too shocked to speak. After a moment, he turned the television on and shook the paper back open. I moved closer to him and asked, keeping my voice calm, "Would you like some red wine?"

"No, thank you."

That night, I slept in the room next to ours, like he asked. The room was completely white and unfurnished except the bed, which gave me the feeling that I'd gone insane.

We began addressing each other with the formal *usted*, which didn't especially bother me. I cooked his meals, ironed his clothes, behaved like the wife I had always been. From the outside, it looked like nothing had changed.

There was a day when he came home from work and I kissed him harder than usual, then wrapped my arms around him and said, "I love you," using *tú* rather than *usted*. He shook me off, though not right away.

"Please," he said, "leave me alone. I'm tired."

Later, Silvia told me, "Úrsula, I don't see how this can continue."

"I don't mind."

"Fine, but I don't want to come to your house this weekend. It would make me too uncomfortable."

"Whatever you like, Silvia."

Víctor was waiting at the table when I got home. He'd already poured me a cup of coffee. "I had coffee with Silvia earlier."

"I don't care where you were, but I'd like you to sit with me for a minute. Have you been crying?"

"No."

"You didn't put on a watch today. Did you get your nails done?"

I was wearing long sleeves, and I had no idea how he could tell whether I had a watch on. He always noticed when I changed some detail: got a manicure, wore different perfume, tried a new lip liner.

I took the full cup of coffee and poured it down the drain. He went to the closet and sat with the door open to show me that he was waiting.

I sat down in the closet with my book and a glass of wine, and, as usual, Víctor turned off his Discman and asked to see what I was reading. He flipped through the book, resting his head on his hand, and then gave me the smile that meant he'd found something he thought I would like.

"Here, Úrsula. You must love this sentence. 'I think that's the danger of keeping a diary: you exaggerate; you spy on yourself; you start rewriting the truth.' Would you like to know how I know?"

His voice was clear and persuasive. I was perfectly aware that he was telling me he read my diary. I tried to look indifferent, like always. I knew perfectly well that he hated indifference. The truth is, I was always paying attention to him.

One afternoon, I had decided to tear all the blank pages out of my books. I knew he'd notice, since he's so highly attuned to detail, and now, as he looked through the novel I was reading, he saw that the white pages at its start and end weren't there. He didn't speak; he made a bitter face and threw the book so it almost hit me in the face.

I smiled slightly, and he said, "You hate me, Úrsula. Right?"

"No, Víctor. I don't hate you."

"So you love me?"

"Yes, I love you."

"But you want to drive me insane. Correct?"

"Víctor, you went crazy all on your own. You went crazy when you decided we had to sit in the closet. Or was it when you started kissing me on the right hand instead of the mouth? Or when you made me sleep alone?"

"You want me to go crazy. You tear the pages out of your books. You call me *usted*. You sleep in the guest bedroom—"

"Because I love you, Víctor! I did that because you asked!"

"That's indifference, Úrsula. You never argue. Never. And you know that I hate indifference."

The closet door was cracked open, and I could feel the cold coming in. Above me, the plastic sequins on one of my dresses glittered like fake little stars. Looking straight at them annoyed me, and so I closed my eyes and sat there in silence.

Plastic

Because I'm lonely, I'm always looking for ways to connect with people. For example, I've taught myself to buy cheap, mass-market books, and only bestsellers, to make it more likely that I'll run into someone reading the same book and be able to start a conversation about it.

I've also started buying things that are strange or elaborate, like Tamagotchis and marionettes, because I don't want just anyone to pay attention to me, but someone who's complicated, who considers his options, takes apart what he sees, someone who can figure out who I am.

But my efforts to find company wear me out. I forget who I'm supposed to be, how to choose what I want, not what I think other people might have.

I'm carrying a bottle of sparkling water. It's a common brand, and I'm sure plenty of people are carrying the same one, but this time I got it because I was thirsty, because I cared more about sparkling water than about company.

She sits next to me with a bottle in her hand. Not water; an energy drink, the caffeinated kind, bright green. I wait for her to open her bottle, and seconds later I open mine. She smiles and there we are on the bus, drinking from bottles that for all I knew were recycled from the same plastic. Our drinks are the same size. Half a liter of liquid slides down each of our throats and our stomachs swell at the same time, like choreographed balloons.

I close the bottle and cup it in my hands like a fragile animal. She closes hers too but holds it tight in her fist. With her free hand she plays with the cap, tries to peel off the fish-toothed plastic that was once its seal for freshness.

The fish teeth are gentle on my fingertips, and while she plays with the plastic, I let myself sink into the sea. She stops playing with the strip of plastic and studies it. She peers into the bottle and the focus in her eyes fills the whole bus, or at least, fills me. Her focus is heavy in my throat, in my stomach. Right away she puts the open bottle between her thighs, holds it with her leg muscles in flowered fabric as she runs her fingers over the ridged cap. The soda she has left jumps against the sides of the bottle. She takes the cap in her hands, thumbs the seal, stretches and twists it, pulls at the plastic like she's a child who's caught a rat by the tail.

The blue plastic turns white and the toothed strip is about to break, and so am I. She puts the seal in her mouth and bites it away from the cap in one try. She pushes a thread of toothed plastic along her tongue, lowers her head, and spits as hard as she can, turning her lungs and throat into an air gun. The strip of plastic flies onto the floor of the bus, and as she removes the bottle from between her thighs to take another drink, she steps on it.

The Woman, completely drunk, collapses on the sofa. The room's thin walls shake. A thread of saliva extends from her lips to the floor. She breathes hard.

The Boy, recently bathed, hair still wet, sits at the table with a blue notebook and a freshly sharpened pencil. He sneezes.

The Man carefully combs the Boy's hair and sprays him with cologne. The air changes for a moment, from sour liquor to lavender. The Man sighs.

"Dad, what does ego mean?"

The Mother mumbles something. She's trying to get comfortable on the sofa but moving gives her the hiccups. The Man puts a bucket of water near the sofa where she's about to pass out. Then he returns to the Boy.

"Ego. Ego is an Armani aftershave. I have a bottle in the bathroom. When I use it before I go out, I can tell people like how it smells. Everyone looks at me, especially women, smiling and breathing in the good-smelling air around me. Ego smells very good."

The Boy takes the pencil and writes in his blue notebook, *Sentence 1. My dad smells like Ego. Women like how he smells.*

The Woman hiccups again. The Man pushes the

bucket closer to her mouth and wipes the sweat from her forehead. It's almost a caress.

"Asshole," she says. "Son of a bitch." Then she pukes.

The sleeve of the Man's shirt is covered in vomit. The Boy writes in his notebook, *Sentence 2*. He puts the pencil down and turns to his father. His eyes are full of tears.

Here and There

Type B

Once I had to go to the doctor because I had such dark circles under my eyes.

The nurses asked me questions and gave me forms to fill out. They asked me to draw myself, then a house, then a tree. They put a tuning fork on my forehead and asked what I felt. I said I felt it vibrating because that's what I was supposed to say, but the truth was that I felt the cold metal and I felt a musical note spiraling into my brain, intense and unending, moving through me while I stared at the doctor's white coat.

After a few days I went back to the clinic and they told me that I was Type B. It sounded like they'd diagnosed me with inferiority, and I was upset when I heard it. I wasn't sure what it meant to be Type B, but I was sure that Type A was better. Then the doctor explained that people who are Type B are night people. They're more productive after dark, and they respond better to moonlight than to sun.

"I see," I said, and then he explained that it's not bad to be Type B. It's just like I'm living in a faraway time zone, like I was somewhere in Asia, and it's true that I've always wanted to travel east. I thought they'd send me home and that would be that, but the doctor told me I should try to become Type A.

I'm not sure it would be better to be Type A, I thought, but it would be nice not to have those dark circles. People would ask me fewer questions. Plus, it would help me get a job.

I tried to follow the doctor's instructions in order to become Type A. I managed it for a few weeks, during which I found a job because I put on a suit and straightened my hair for the interview and didn't have dark circles under my eyes. Once I had the job, though, I went back to my Type B ways.

The problem for a Type B living where I do, in the Arctic Circle, is that I need darkness to be productive and during the white nights I produce nothing. I get distracted by the light. I watch the dust float and imagine the stars I can't see. In my head the stars watch me as I try to fall asleep. They watch as I stare into the luminous sky, at the clouds that hang over me day after day. The stars think I'm looking at them, but the truth is, I'm just finding shapes in the clouds.

Plasticine Dreams

It seems the cold, dark winter has ended. Today, finally, it felt like spring. I sat on a park bench waiting for something to happen and, like always, something did: I heard a lawn mower.

A boy my age appeared suddenly and began cutting the grass with a machine I'd never seen before. It wasn't the usual machine, the one you have to push while you walk across the lawn. This was more interesting. It was a tube with a propeller on one end, and as the propeller whirled it cut the grass at high speed. The kid was an artist, a grass stylist. He held the tube level and, with a firm hand, glided it slowly over the grass. His movements were so smooth and perfect that he seemed part of the machine. It seemed he extended his arm and, magically, the grass cut itself. He walked up and down the park, tracing his own path several times, like me pacing my house. At the end, he'd left the grass completely even. It looked like the head of a young soldier who's just joined the army, his green hair newly buzzed.

I applauded from my bench. I wanted to thank him for his magic trick. He gestured to the machine, then put a hand on his stomach and bowed, like an actor before the curtain falls.

Then the second act began.

The kid returned with a similar machine, another tube, but this time he wore a strange sort of backpack. It was a vacuum. He collected the cut grass in the backpack, and I watched him trace his steps around the park, entertaining myself with the vision of the cut grass flying into the machine like green rain. When he was done, he emptied the contents of his backpack into a sack and twisted it shut.

I applauded again and he bowed like before, then disappeared.

I'd gone to the theater by mistake.

Then came the smell of cut grass, which I've always loved. Every time someone mows a lawn, that smell spreads everywhere, turning the whole world green and new. It's like we're all wrapped in the freshly clipped grass. I stayed a while, breathing deeply, storing the greenness inside me, like a line from a poem: *Green body, green hair.*

(Photosynthesis)

•

In the part of the year when it never gets dark, the plants are constantly active. They can't rest. Sap flows through their veins and stems all day. Chlorophyll courses, sticks to their pores, spreads through the air. It happens to me, too. In spring, my blood moves violently, and my physical activity—and mental, which at times I still have—speeds to a wild gallop. Then my rampant insomnia begins.

The last time this happened, I stayed awake so long that the skin on my head went numb. When I looked in the mirror, I saw an illustration from the anatomy books I like so much. I saw my veins and arteries defined perfectly, and brilliant blood streaming through them while I moved. I saw my muscles holding back this torrent of blood, like dikes on the banks of a river. My thoughts filled with clouds and a thick veil of fog covered my eyes, obscuring the world around me. The vertigo kept going. Light entered me like a wave, and photosynthesis began. Fluid moved through the roots of my body, through every nerve and joint, filling me from stem to leaf. I was a plant. I moved myself into a stream of cold water for a few minutes, feeling the weight of each drop on my skull. The water ran down my neck and face, over my cold eyes, like it had turned into my own exhaustion, my prolonged vigil, like it had become liquid thought. I was soaked in thought. Thoughts sank into my pores and pooled in my feet, warm now, part of my blood, whirling through me in an eternal spiral.

•

In the park I can see the grass growing, sped-up and sleepless, like me in the spring.

A green plasticine giant appears in my head. His steps don't make any sound, but his thick green footsteps appear in the grass, spreading like some dense, soft mass that sticks to the ground. He takes a lawn mower from his pocket, the same as the one I just saw, and I watch him begin to trim the other plants and trees. I lie on the bench and look closely at the grass, which has become a multitude of green humans, insomniacs, standing and praying for sleep. The giant walks over them, cutting off their heads one by one. With every slice, there's a drop of blood.

A girl sees him from her bench and applauds. The giant takes her in his hands and rocks her until she falls asleep. The two of them breathe the smell of blood together.

The bench feels as soft as the giant's belly, and I stretch and climb to my feet. I've seen a lot today. I think I'm ready to sleep.

Fish

When people talk about the smells of their childhood, most of them talk about coffee, freshly baked bread, chocolate, new notebooks, and just-sharpened pencils. I could talk about those smells, too, but I was born and grew up (and once died) in Lima, and so my childhood is marked by another smell: dead fish.

Lima smells like fish.

I remember how the smell arrived before the sun, so strong that it woke me up some days. As we ate breakfast, the smell became thick, almost solid, turning the dark mornings the color of a cleaned fish, of steel hooks wrapped in gills and tripe. I remember looking at the fish-smell sky while my mother packed my lunch, an early-rising cuckoo singing in the background.

The smell touched everything. It got under our skin.

At school we made faces at each other, grimacing,

revolted but laughing, since in childhood, disgust always leads to laughter. It's only with age that we learn to treat disgust seriously, that sometimes the right response to disgust is rage.

Wrapped in our gray uniforms, we sat in the humid patio and talked about the smell. We said it came from a fishmeal factory, and that while we were at recess, somewhere else an infinite line of fish was getting chopped to bits with enormous knives, guts and scales flying from the conveyor belt into the factory workers' eyes. Someone said no, the factory made the fish we had to eat at home, and we laughed again, flattening our child mouths in disgust.

I once heard a poet say that Lima smells like a whore. I was still in primary school, and after that our morning discussions of fish smell had a new component: whore smell. When you're young it's hard to imagine a whore. You can recognize them because you know they wear low-cut dresses and stand on street corners, but you can't understand what they do. At recess we worked on our knowledge of prostitutes. Some of my classmates said the fish smell came from their mouths. Others thought it came from their sweat, and a few better-informed claimed it started between their legs.

I remember a morning one winter when the smell was so strong it was news.

The sea had spat out thousands of fish. They

covered the shore, each one a scale of a giant fish beached on the Peruvian coast.

The fish were dark, and shone blue and silver, like metal. I remember how they looked on our JVC television, full color, with a remote control. We'd gotten it brand-new that year.

I watched people in bright clothes go to the beaches with bright buckets to collect the fish. Everyone went home happy, buckets full, and I imagined them feasting for months, eating ceviche, sudado, escabeche, croquettes, fish with garlic. . .

"Mamá," I said. "We should go get fish on the beach, too."

My mother, when she replied, sounded very serious. "What are you thinking? When the sea spits out fish, it means they were sick. These fish are rotten inside."

I kept watching the people on the news, smiling with their buckets of fish. Some were interviewed while standing barefoot among the fish, sweating and covered with scales. They said this was their second trip to the shore, that they'd eaten the fish and it was good, it was delicious, there was no danger at all.

I didn't want to eat the fish anymore, but I wanted to know how it felt to bury my feet in them. I wanted to touch the rejected fish, slip on their fat bodies and sharp scales. I wanted to let the fish into my pores, to roll in them, breathe in their smell, which was the smell of Lima. I wanted the fish smell inside me for good. Mostly, I wanted to see them. I wanted to look at the miles of beached fish, stretching down the shore like the dead on D-Day. I wanted to see whether all the fish were truly dead. Maybe a few were alive, flapping their gills.

I never saw them. I never found out.

I never knew whether the city government cleaned up the fish or the people did. For a long time, I imagined them rotting, and later I imagined people picking up the skeletons to make bracelets or necklaces.

From then on, my childhood smelled of fish and whores. It's marked by the day of the fish, which had such a big impact on me as a child. It thrilled me then, but as the years go by, it's turned into a sad, dark story.

When I see the fish through adult eyes, I see a poor country that grinned through a crisis; a country that celebrated the chance to collect beached fish on a winter morning because those fish would feed so many families. The image of the fish returns in my head, and I disappear into a tangle of pain, picturing all the bodies beached by terrorism in the sierra, the poor and the dead who crossed the screen of the color television all those mornings of my childhood, and who return now, like a postcard from Lima, full of indifference and pain.

I Remember

I remember that once my mother had to go on a trip for a few days, and when she said goodbye, she gave me a stuffed monkey to keep me company till she got home.

I would have been four then, and I carried that monkey around until I was ten or eleven. It was a gray monkey, with plastic hands and feet, plastic ears, a plastic face, and thumbs shaped to fit inside its ears or up its nose.

I remember my mother's closet full of office supplies, too. Sometimes she and I would go in there looking for God knows what and end up organizing all the papers and thumbtacks and notepads she had.

I inherited a lot from my mother. The way I laugh, and the ability to speak in code. Sometimes, all we need is one word and some context to get a whole message across. I have my mother's eyes, too. Not the shape, but the sight. Like my mother, I notice even the smallest details around me.

I often think about my mother in the mornings. I think about her, about what she did in her life. Like the time she volunteered in the mountains, in Huaraz, in the seventies. There had been an earthquake. She slept in a tent for months, carried blankets and clothes, cooked meals for the badly injured. I think about her while I drink my coffee every morning, inevitably, because in Lima she was the one who made coffee for me.

Remembering my childhood is like opening a drawer full of photos. Songs, too, and smells, and words.

My grandmother is there too, my grandmother who I remember so well I can feel her.

I remember how she did my hair before school. She braided it perfectly, pulling the braids tight, tying them with white satin ribbons as she said, "You have so much hair. You must have gotten that from me."

Before she started to comb my hair, she always soaked it with cold water, patting my head with her wet palms, which she said would refresh my brain and help the lessons get in. After all this time I've forgotten the lessons, but not the cold water, not the splash of her hands on my head.

I remember waking up at midnight and running to my mother's room. If she wasn't there—she traveled for work—I'd run to the guest room, to whoever was staying with me, my grandmother or my aunt. My mother would sing me "Mi Niña Veneno," *medianoche en mi cuarto, ella va a subir, oigo sus pasos acercándose, veo la puerta abrir*, that song about a girl's footsteps at midnight, a girl slamming a door open, like me.

She had a red VW Beetle and she drove me everywhere, letting me choose which tape to play. I remember the windshield filling with Lima's weak fog, the wiper coming and going, pushing the dirty rain away while we listened to Lionel Richie, the Police, José José, Raphael. She'd take me for ice cream in the Botica Francesa del Jirón de la Unión, which isn't there anymore (which tells you my age), and talk to me as if I were an adult. She'd say, "When you have a daughter . . ." as the waiter brought me a sundae the size of my four-year-old head.

I remember how Lima looked in the eighties: empty, always gray, with fewer people than today, and less noise, I think, because all I heard were the songs I always had in my head.

I still wake up at midnight. Sometimes I get out of bed and listen to the sound of my footsteps on the wood floor until the memory of my childhood comes running back like a frightened child. My stuffed monkey opens the door, and in come my mother, my braids tugging at my temples, my aunt, the cold water in Lima's humid air, my grandmother, the school smells of paper and books. My childhood cuts a hole through my memory, aches as it works its way to the surface, then stands before me, alive. Then I sit with my memory in the living room, drink a glass of water, and listen to that song with the volume turned low.

me veo hablando con paredes hasta anochecer . . . mi niña veneno, tú tienes un modo sereno de ser . . .

And I think about the days you want your childhood back, all of it, how the longing hits on a night like any other, when you're twenty-six years old and can't sleep, when you're in your pajamas, all alone.

I Don't Remember

I forgot how the mornings sound here: the newscasters' accents, the forks rattling in bars that serve breakfast, the exhausted waitresses with their quick feet. I forgot the grown men drinking out of child-sized cups, the pastry smells: *ensaimadas, napolitanas, flautas, churros*. I forgot all the people in a hurry who sit down and eat in peace.

I forgot Valencia orange juice. I forgot the little sandwiches that get their own moment. I forgot the long loaves of bread, which these days I call *baguettes*. I forgot about tapas and Mercadona wine and the apartment on Visitación where no one ever visited us. I forgot the Benimaclet metro stop and all the plates I washed and all the plates I left in the sink. I forgot the words *sofrito, hucha,* and *consumición*. I forgot the stand that sold comics I never read, and the literature department, and Esther and Mireia and Raquel and Pilar. I forgot you.

I forgot the neighborhoods, Carmen and Viveros,

and the Turia River that looked like a Sorolla painting, and all those nameless downtown streets that only
existed at night. I forgot the VWs charging through traf-
fic, the avenues where my steps sounded like I was running away, the Vespas on which I held onto your waist
and never wore a helmet. I forgot the sick pigeons in
the plazas, the old men, the Ramblas full of cafes and
angels, the ghosts, the Dalís and Picassos and Cernudas
and Gaudís on the corners. I forgot my dead because I
was too busy being alive. I forgot the churches that look
like ours and the newsstands where I bought *El País*
even though it wasn't my country. I forgot how to say
buenos días, venga, vale, hasta ahora.

I forgot the glasses of beer, the hours I spent, peseta
by peseta, in the bar on the corner. I forgot the hours getting drunk for nothing and laughing so loudly you could
have heard me from my house. I forgot the bottles of wine
I drank while I cried, all that Rioja while I fell out of love,
all the sweat that smelled like wet wood and anise.

I forgot the foreign whores who called everybody
cariño, even the ones who walked by my house every day
when I lived downtown. I forgot the junkies asking for
change to buy beer and cigarettes, the 100-peseta stores,
the Chinese stores, the Arab stores, the cost of life,
the long line of foreigners where you waited to ascend
to legal status, better than heaven. I forgot the phone
booths where we shut ourselves up to cry on long-distance calls. I forgot that country of immigrants plucked

from the water, fallen from the sky, that brightly colored country tacked onto a peninsula far away.

I forgot the pills, the tobacco, the doctors, the cots and futons, the nightstands, the other sides of the bed, the relatives, the neighbors. I forgot myself.

I forgot the Mediterranean kisses, the Valencian hugs. I forgot that I'd made love in Spanish. I forgot the love I hung on the wall to dry, packed in salt, waiting in silence and darkness like a leg of Iberian ham.

I forgot the names of the trains that took me everywhere. I forgot the phone numbers, the missed calls, the answering machines full of ashes, I forgot how much earlier it was in the Canary Islands, I forgot *quarter of* and *twenty of* and all the ways to say I'm running late. I forgot there are holes in the coins, and a thousand pesetas is six euros, and two and a half years in Spain is my other life, but sometimes I remember for a moment in the middle of the night that those years were my whole life, that they're everything I have.

I didn't remember that piece of Iberia that I carry inside me, as if I were some medieval hero. I'll never be able to get it out. It's like a thorn buried deep in my flesh.

I didn't remember that I liked Hombres G.

Then I put on this album and they told me, *yo no tengo a nadie sobre quién escribir*. I don't have anyone to write about.

That's why I wrote all this down.

Placebo

*

the crash test dummy: a story of love and desire
(take 1)
I'm driving too fast at the place where Route 25 curves
and I crash.

at impact I break into seven parts. seven like the
day I was born. my biggest accident.

two legs + two arms + one torso + one head + one
heart

seven

I break into pieces and there's my crash test heart

desire smashes my heart into a wall and love is
there filming everything.

speed, intensity, acceleration, impact.

my voice when the camera's off: see how even
though she had her seatbelt on, the damage is very
bad.
(take 2)
I'm a dummy made of seven naked parts on white
hotel sheets.

this time the curve is the curve the key makes in
the lock on the hotel room door

I don't make a noise, I just go to the door, open it
and there's an explosion and I fall apart.

my shaky voice when the camera's off: this has been devastating.

I leave the room a mess. my uninjured lover is still asleep in the white sheets and the clock is still ticking on the wall.

Placebo for Bleeding to Death

1. Think about this. In the García Márquez story "The Trail of Your Blood in the Snow," newlywed Nena Daconte dies on her honeymoon. One of the roses in her bouquet pricks her ring finger and she bleeds to death.

Her blood leaves a trail down the highway from Paris to Madrid.

One line of blood for miles.

2. Two days ago I had a headache like a surgeon.

First it sliced through the skin around my left eye. Then it peeled away muscles, separated nerves, gripped my eye in its socket, and squeezed until my head split like a walnut. It broke the protective film around my brain and left all my thoughts exposed.

Then the pain started to move. It flickered like a neon sign trapped in the window of an empty bar. On, off, on. An intermittent pain.

The pain was like a wind inside my head. It dried all my thoughts to nothing.

It was pain like kerosene on wood, like dry heat scraping my skin. It was pain like a mind full of splinters.

3. There are mornings when you get up and your body hurts like last night you binged on pain. Your limbs are so heavy it's like your blood has turned to mercury. It's as if you're trapped in an explosion, no, an explosion is trapped inside of you. You can't hear. Your eyes are dry sockets. Your hands are hot and empty and your thoughts burn up like gas.

You go through your day like this, in pieces, your silk scarf and your best jacket soaked with pain.

4. Sometimes people bleed to death in front of me and no one else notices. Yesterday I saw a girl bleeding in the cafeteria.

She was eating a salad, talking with a woman at her table and a man who might have been her husband. Their rings matched, anyway.

Blood dripped over the sides of the chair. It soaked into her purple sweater, dripped from her ponytail, ran down the seams of her pants.

My table was across from hers and so I could see it all.

Every so often she stopped talking, cut her bread

with a knife, mopped up salad dressing and ate the bread in bits, staring into space.

She stayed quiet for a while, looking into the cafeteria's kitchen, while her companions kept talking. Then she got up and walked to the water fountain.

She left a trail of blood on the cafeteria floor. She got three cups, filled them with water, and put them on a tray.

She came back.

She drank the water very quickly, urgently, as if it was saving her life. Then she started to bleed more. The liquid was thinner and paler. The rest of the dark dehydrated blood came out in a rush, followed by water.

She stretched her legs, let her arms fall to her sides, slid down in her chair until her neck touched its back, where she'd hung her blood-stained jacket.

After a while the three got up. She put on her jacket and kept bleeding.

I spent the whole afternoon thinking about her, how she'd stared into space, her three glasses of water, her long steps toward the water fountain while she was bleeding to death. There was no way she'd survive the afternoon.

5. When you take a painkiller, you know that your headache will be gone in less than forty-five minutes.

During that time all you think about is the pain.

You wait for it to end. You try to focus on something else, but all you can do is lie down, close your eyes, and let the chemicals take effect.

I've read that this waiting period, when you're certain that your pain will lift soon, that knowledge that you have less than forty-five more minutes of pain to get through, makes the painkillers stronger. It's called the placebo effect.

A doctor could give you chalk and tell you it's a headache cure, and you'd take it, lie down to wait, and, sooner or later, the pain would be gone. All you'd have taken was belief.

Knowing there's a cure is the cure.

*

This girl came in today and I think she might be an angel. Her cold body on the steel bed upsets me, but I can't stop looking. She committed suicide with rum and rat poison. When I opened her eyes, I saw light. When I touched her hands, they were cold, but they moved. Her fingers were soft, docile. Where her lips part there's still some saliva. It looks like silver. I know she's an angel. Angels are everywhere. In the morgue's cafeteria they're saying that she was a prostitute. They're saying she arrived in a tight, low-cut dress. Sons of bitches. They say you could see how the dress pushed up her tits; they say you could see her ass clearly defined through the fabric. I've seen her naked. Her body was just a gray shadow on the bright steel. It stood out in the cold air of the freezer room. She's an angel, I'm telling you. No one's come to pick her up. Angels are always alone. Angels don't have families.

Take Charge

We need someone to take charge of our souls.

I woke up with that line in my head today. If I'd had somebody in bed with me, I would have rolled over and, instead of good morning, said, "We need someone to take charge of our souls," and then yawned.

While I brushed my teeth with my eyes closed, I thought, we need someone to take charge of our souls.

It's stayed in my head all day, hammering through my grocery list.

List:
- cream
- strawberries
- orange juice
- tomatoes
- champagne
- ham

- we need someone to take charge of our souls
- laundry detergent
- napkins
- broccoli
- tampons (?)

Summer vacation is ending, and I keep running into people who are just back from trips. They always start talking about where they've been while we're stand in line at the supermarket, listening to the register spitting out change, watching the conveyor belt spool past with the things we use to fill our houses and lives: jam to spread on our toast, then turn into blood sugar; detergent to watch secrets out of our sheets; paper to write lines, lies, and lists on, to keep ourselves from forgetting, as if we could forget; canned vegetables to outlive us; butter and cheese in plastic tubs to save till we die because we might need them for storage someday.

It's not like we ever have leftovers.

We need someone to take charge of our souls. Wrap them in plastic, at least.

I heard two people talking in the supermarket today, one telling the other about a trip to Thailand, talking about how prostitutes grab you by the shirt there, you're just walking down the street and they're on you like lizards, telling you that you have to come home with them, or else you're taking a piss in a bar bathroom and one locks herself in with you and tells you that you have to take her home, and the bathroom, no, all of Bangkok smells like shit, I'm not kidding, it's not that it smells bad, it's that it smells like shit.

I turned to see the tourist's face, and he must have slept with a thousand whores in Thailand, because there's no way anyone would touch him here.

—don't be cruel—

He looked dirty. He was thin and white, but not pink-white like most people here; he was halfway between gray and violet. His teeth were small and dirty, like a rat that just finished a piece of moldy cheese.

I imagined him fucking a prostitute, imagined her turning away when he was done, telling him, "You need someone to take charge of your soul," as she got dressed and tucked his money between her breasts.

We need someone to take charge of our souls.

—poor rat—

I drove home at exactly the speed limit. Everything was perfect.

(Except my thoughts; except me.)

"No Rain" was playing on the radio. That's what my life was like in those days.

I don't understand why I sleep all day / And I start to complain that there's no rain / And all I can do is read a book to stay awake / and it rips my life away, but it's a great escape

Later I imagined that there had been a terrible

accident in my peaceful city. The accident was so bad that it appeared in every newspaper in the world.

I was there, in the accident. Somewhere in the wreckage, with the dead and the wounded, there I was.

I saw myself with my forehead bleeding, my hands torn, my cheek flat against the pavement.

I saw God and the Devil coming out of their hiding place by the highway.

Trapped in the iron maze of my imagination, I thought: We need someone to take charge of our souls.

God closed the eyes of the dead with a kiss and the Devil started shouting at the injured, slapping them awake.

Red light.

(devil's eyes)

I caught myself.

I need someone to take charge of my soul.

Oppfølgingstjenesten

After you've been in a mental hospital longer than a college semester, getting out isn't as easy as picking up a prescription and kissing your shrink goodbye. The nurses don't just wave you out the door. No, they assign someone to follow you, to, as they say, finish the job. The person is called your *oppfølgingstjenesten*, which means following-service-man, or something like that, and on paranoid days you might start to believe that he or she is following you for real, you see her everywhere you go, and so you begin trying to avoid telling her much about your life, although every so often on a sunny day you agree to have coffee with her and find yourself telling her that you're only crying because it's autumn, or that you don't need so many pills these days, that you don't want to take them anymore.

The truth is that I don't think I need anyone to follow me or take care of me. My cat takes care of me, and my days follow me around, all perfectly recorded, impossible to escape, even when I turn off my computer and phone. Look at them: the newspapers, my calendar, my Facebook page, all those receipts.

But even though I've been out for months, Laila still follows me, her blue eyes wide open. Every so often I call her and say this isn't necessary, and after that I don't see her for weeks, but then there are times when I send her a message saying what's up? busy this week? and she knows I might be falling apart and so she responds right away, always with smiley faces, and we make a date.

Laila comes to my house smiling. She always hugs me when she arrives. I like her, even though I see her inspecting my floorboards, noticing today that instead of the usual shine they're covered with paint. She'll make a note of it, I know. Paint stains on the floorboards, cat hair, clean smell, clean clothes, empty bottles. I bet she writes down everything she sees.

What's strange about Laila is that she has lots of psychiatric patients, people she helps and takes care of, but she believes in extraterrestrials, in the energies of the universe, in crystals, in shamans. I tell her that not taking my meds feels good some of the time, but when it feels bad, it's awful, and the worst part is that it makes me eat all this sugar. She tells me that there are quartzes that will give me balance, and that meditation helps, too.

I would rather have her increase my dosage of

quartzes than increase my dosage of prescribed medication. Still, it's strange.

Recently Laila told me that the autumn wind carries away our burdens like it does dead leaves. I listened and smiled. I'm starting to wonder if Laila's still following me. I think I might be following her.

*

Today in bed, waiting for my fever to go down, I imagined that I was a country.

I imagined that everyone who lived in my body was hearing on TV or reading in the newspaper that there was a heat wave.

I began to feel a buzzing in my body, like all the people inside were moving around, searching for someplace cooler.

They arrived at my palms, which were sweaty and cold.

I had thousands of overheated citizens on my hands, in sun hats and loose summer clothes. They seemed lonely, and sad, and a little ridiculous, as big groups on the beach often do.

I closed my fists and killed them all.

They turned into mercury.

I was an abandoned nation.

Tom

His name is Tom. It's an unusual name in Norway, because in Norwegian *tom* means:

tom   II **tom** adj. (norr *tómr*)
1. som r uten innhold
   t-me hyller / postkassa er t- / arbeide på t- mage uten å ha spist / starte med to t-me hender på bar bakke / *gå t- for bensin* slippe opp for bensin
2. uten inventor; ubebodd, øde
   et t-t rom / huset har stått t-t i over et år / folket- / det ble t-t etter dem de ble savnet
3. uten rot I virkeligheten, verdiløs
   t-me beskyldninger, løfter, trusler / t-me fraser
4. som r uten initiativ, som r uten skapende kraft
   kjenne seg t- innvendig / voere t- for ideer / et t-t blikk, smil.

Let me translate.

<u>tom</u> adj.

1. without content

   empty shelves / empty mailbox / empty stomach / empty hands

2. without material or tangible goods, without inhabitants, empty, abandoned

   empty room / abandoned house / abandoned child

3. without roots, without basis in reality, without value

   baseless accusations / worthless promises / empty words

4. without initiative, without ability, without creativity, not constructive

   running out of ideas / an empty look / an empty smile

For me, Tom is everything the dictionary describes. He's like an empty bucket I can vomit in, pee in, bleed in, that I can fill with my darkest self. Tom acts like a man with no home or family. He must have come from somewhere, he must have a mother or father who named him Tom, or maybe he chose the name for himself. I admit that I Googled him once. I found out that he'd participated in a hiking marathon here; he'd climbed the seven hills of Bodø. It's the only sign I have that he engages with the rest of society. He has a hobby; he made a commitment; he must be human.

He always wears black. I don't know if it's his favorite color, or if he's ever put on jeans, or traditional Norwegian dress. I don't know if he has a body under his black suit, if he has hair and bones and blood, if he ever spits or sleeps or eats.

Tom is a son, I guess. He might be a father, or a grandfather. He's a person like me. He writes with a pen. He collects strange objects and paints pictures.

Tom sits in a chair and I sit on the couch. We're next to each other. We never make eye contact. I try not to touch his hands when I pay him for 45 minutes of psychoanalysis. Sometimes when I arrive at his office, I'm furious and want to talk about how angry I am, but he always asks questions, or says things like "Your cat is a little killing machine," and so I have to say that it's instinct, and besides, my cat is my friend, not my child, not my husband. I don't know how to do it, how the conversation should go, and so before the session's done, I'm trying to translate Eielson poems into Norwegian, and after that, we talk about death.

D.

~~Dear~~ D.
I'm done with you.

D. is for:

~~Dear~~
~~Darling~~
Distress
Disguise
Discomfort
Deception
Depression
Despair
Defense
Dogma
Defeat
Disgrace
Dinginess
Defection
Dominant
Dad
Drink
Disgust
Disaster
Departure

Drastic
Disagreement
Disenchantment
Dirt
Demand
Discussion
Discredit
Doubt
Disrespect
Denial
Disapproval
Distance
Divorce
Disappearance
Discord
Disappointment
Detachment
Dullness
Devil
Dog

You changed my routines but not my plans. You cleaned my kitchen but dirtied the rest of my house. You tricked me with your accent but helped build my vocabulary. You reminded me of that one Elvis song I forgot.

~~Dear~~ D. It was good while it lasted, but it's good that it didn't last (long).

But I got wise, my ~~dear~~ D. My devil in disguise.

*

You know how DVDs come with director's commentary? It would be nice if books did, too. You could have a little knife and headphones, and when you cut open a word, you'd hear the author saying, "In this line, the word canvas means more than just a cloth the protagonist paints on. When I wrote canvas, I saw a huge blank space, a space where anything can happen. You'll see, in chapter 15, when the canvas breaks, the characters have no more space to breathe. They're in agony after that. It's like they're drowning in their own history."

Then the author would start to cry, and you'd take off your headphones and put away your knife.

Or you'd keep listening, and you'd hear the author burst out laughing. You'd hear the author say, "Don't get upset. The whole thing's a lie. It's like a kaleidoscope, or a stereogram. Just a bunch of shit layered together so it looks nice."

(Better, no?)

Blood and Water

Swimming Pool

There are more swimming pools in France than in any other European country. Almost 100 people drown in French pools every year.

We go to the pool in order not to exist.

I go when I'm sick of everything, when the weight of my own body exhausts me, when I can't stand to hear my own steps on the sidewalk.

In the water, I'm weightless. I float like a corpse, and when I get out, I'm ready to be alive.

When I was young my mother and I used to spend a lot of time in the living room, coming up with possible answers to questions like whether there's life in outer space. We always watched shows like *Ripley's Believe It or Not*, and at the end, my mother would turn off the TV and ask me if I thought there was life on other planets. I never had an answer, but we'd sit in silence for a long time. Then my mother served dinner, and once we sat down the silence was done. We came up with so many answers at that table.

Ripley's Believe It or Not isn't on anymore, and my mother and I don't ask so many questions. We just talk. We're two women at a kitchen table, drinking in each other's words and silences with each sip of coffee, the room still full of answers after all this time.

But when I'm alone, I still have questions without answers, and when I think about them too long, I fall apart. That's another reason I go to the pool.

Water has always given me a sense of order. Something about the surface tension, the way it changes with the temperature, the arrangement of its molecules: two hydrogen and one oxygen, a broken triangle, a balance. The water cycle reminds me there's harmony out there, and clarity, and calm—though sometimes, during storms, it's more like a person shouting the truth.

The molecules in a liquid both attract and repel each other. The molecules on the surface of that liquid tend to order themselves such that the surface behaves as if it were contained by an invisible membrane. We call this surface tension. Liquids form spherical drops due to surface tension. It enables blood to move toward the heart. It prevents objects from entering bodies of water; in other words, it means we can float.

Water helps when I'm falling apart, and it helps with my questions. When I'm in the pool, I become part of the water. It's as if I left my skin in the locker room, like he liquids that flow through me don't need a body; they can stay together without my body and its exhausting weight.

I have a theory: people who need answers, like me, look for them at the bottoms of pools, where there's order.

Though sometimes we just do the dead man's float, too. What can I say? Life is tiring.

Today I watched everyone swim from the bleachers. Each stroke seemed like a question. Some people swim fast, desperately, sucking in air like each breath might be the answer they need. Others float on their backs, letting the water get into their thoughts, waiting for an answer to form in the air above them as they drift in the other swimmers' wakes.

Depression is linked to a specific point in the brain, not far from the place where we absorb knowledge. To study this further, a group of scientists at the General Hospital of Valencia observes the behavior of rats in a forced-swimming experiment. When the rats are put in the water for the first time, they swim energetically for five minutes. For five more, they swim slowly. After that, they just float until the scientists scoop them from the pool. In the next trial, the rats stop swimming much sooner. They're passive.

After two minutes in the water, they start to float. This is a sign of depression and learned hopelessness.

I remember all the times I've thrown myself violently into the water because I wanted to touch the bottom, to get to the bottom of my sadness. I'd hold my breath and force myself to the tiled floor, thinking about my childhood, my father, my mother, all our silent lights in the living room; I'd think about falling out of love until my chest hurt, and then I'd let all the air go, turning my thoughts to bubbles, and float like a dead body to the surface.

I think we've all wished—at least for a moment, at least once in our lives—not to exist. And we've all gone in search of answers to impossible questions.

This is why pools are so popular.

My pool can be overwhelming. It's too full. There's the chaos of naked bodies in the locker room, and then there are all the bodies in the pool. The water is choppy, like my thoughts. There's uncertainty, chaos, doubt, loneliness. Some days all it has to offer is twenty-five meters of butterfly and the smell of chlorine.

I've been coming to this pool for a year. I was here when it opened. I needed answers, but that day all I got was my reflection in the tiles.

Today I came for an event. The pool's been open one year, and we're celebrating. Two girls who swim in the mornings choreographed an aqua ballet; a few women made lane dividers out of corks and bright plastic; we had a play in which someone pretended to drown; and a very serious man I sometimes swim next to revealed himself to be a chemist and explained how to dechlorinate pool water for reuse.

Now it's my turn.

I said I'd organize a game. I wanted to help everyone get to know our fellow swimmers better, since in the pool we never talk. For the last few days, I've taken pictures in the showers—secretly, of course, so the game would be a surprise—and last night, I cut each one into a three-piece puzzle. The challenge is to put a body together correctly, matching a head to its torso and legs.

But when I introduce myself and start to display my game, everyone jumps from the bleachers and grabs their own parts.

I have to raise my voice to tell them the rules. I take the pictures away from the swimmers to demonstrate, see, you don't complete your own photo. The game is too easy that way.

But no one here is interested in the game. Or else they aren't interested in each other. Everyone takes their own body, but, at the end, mine is gone. All that's left is my head and the wrinkled, drooping torso and legs of the osteoporotic woman who comes to the pool to strengthen her bones.

"Fine," I say. "If you don't want to play, just give

me my body back," but no one listens to me. It's as if I don't exist.

I pick up the photo of my face and decide to leave, but as I'm walking away the osteoporotic woman stops me and announces, "I won!"

She shows me all three parts of a photo. They fit. I look at her naked, shriveled body, and then I hug her and declare her the winner. I even give her the prize: water wings, a snorkel, and red goggles.

Not everybody applauds.

In certain YMCAs, it is considered poor hygiene to wear a bathing suit.

*

Fish out of water don't die from lack of oxygen. Air has plenty of oxygen, much more than water. Fish die because their respiratory system won't operate on land. Their gills stick together. Water flows through their gills, full of oxygen, but air weighs the gills down. Fish on land suffocate. They choke on air.

The Drowning Man

I like how the word *water* sounds. My mother used to
say it was my first word, so I must have liked it even as
an infant.

Here, on the sand with my eyes closed, I can feel
the ocean moving in silence. There's no wind here,
and it doesn't smell like women. Not like in Lima. The
whole world knows that Lima smells like pussy. Here,
there's rarely even a breeze.

Wind here is like rain in Lima.

The rain in Lima is shy. There are people who say
the rain is a hypocrite, but I think it just needs to grow
up. The rain in Lima is a crying teenager, a storm all at
once and then nothing, no explanation. The rain here is
a grown man's lament.

Once I told my doctor that when I heard voices,
first they said my name, then a few words at random.
I suggested that if I wrote down the words, I might be

able to find some hidden message. I told him that I felt intense anxiety when I heard rain on the roof because each drop sounded like one syllable shouted into the tiles. It's a heartrending sound, I told him. Sometimes I go outside to hear the rain shouting, to figure out what it wants to tell me so badly, or just to listen because it sounds so desperate, but all that happens is that I get soaked.

The doctor opened his eyes and picked up his pen with both hands, as if it were very heavy. He held it like that and told me that I was describing symptoms of schizophrenia. He made a note with his heavy pen and then gave me a prescription for pink pills that I'm supposed to take with plenty of water.

I take the pills now, but I'm still miserable and depressed. It's ironic, really.

The irony is that I have a new job in a lab where they do experiments on rats to determine the origins of depression. The scientists put the rats in water, and I think then they just watch them drown. I'm not sure. I guess if the rats drown it's because they're depressed. I just clean the lab and the cages. Sometimes I listen to the researchers' conversations, but it's not like I understand. Today I considered telling them that if they were interested, they could experiment on me instead of the rats.

Poor rats. I've seen them swim, thrashing around, trying not to die under observation. I brought them cheese once when I knew no one was watching. I don't know if giving them food will affect the results of the experiment, but I thought they seemed happy to have it. They were all wet, poor things, but they stopped squeaking while they ate my gorgonzola.

In Lima, when I was a boy, my grandmother made pasteles for me to take to school on days I didn't want to go. They worked for me like cheese for the rats. In Lima I was depressed. I couldn't sleep. There wasn't even rain to listen to.

I'm thinking about water again. I've got a glass of it by the medicine cabinet. It looks dirty, and it's been there for days. I don't know why I don't pour it out. I must be waiting for it to change. Maybe it'll turn green, or start bubbling, or disappear.

I'm getting sunburned now, and it hurts. I pour my bottle of sparking water over my chest and shiver.

I remember my mother ironing my school uniform, flicking jasmine-scented water over the gray cloth. I can hear the hiss of the iron sucking up the perfume. The memory has taken me over.

Blood, semen, sweat, piss, saliva, tears: it's all water. The scientists I work with probably separate the water from all those liquids and guard it in a flask somewhere, like a magic potion. They probably drink it to stay young, or to get stronger. Maybe it erases their problems or cleans their scabbed wounds.

The water companies tell us Water Is Life. Don't

Waste It. The science teachers tell us water takes the form of its container. I need a container, too, but the best I can do is a whore. She's like the flask, and I'm like the scientists' purified water: vulnerable.

The last woman I loved was 70 percent water.

Strange thoughts circle through my mind. Depressed rats in the lab, depressed rats in the sewers. All the women I've known. All my fears. My green glass in the bathroom, bubbles in stagnant water, me swimming laps.

When I open my eyes, the sun's setting. I'm alone on the beach and I'm thirsty.

I walk to the edge of the water, and the waves on my feet feel good enough to make me smile. I watch the orange horizon and sigh. I can hear splashes like the ones I made in the pool as a seven-year-old, kicking my feet from the edge, or when I was even younger, and my mother gave me baths in a yellow plastic tub.

I'm an idiot. I'm a twenty-six-year-old child: ridiculous, half-naked, lost.

Now I can see that the splashes are coming from a drowning man. He's not far from me. He's choking on water like a fish on air. I'm sure fish are thirsty when they're drowning, but is this man thirsty now? I wade into the water up to my chest. I want to help, but I don't know how to swim. It's hopeless. I make my way back to shore. The chorus of a song comes into my head: *Nunca digas que esta agua no beberé.*

I look up and down the beach, but there's no one. Just me and the drowning man.

I settle down on the wet sand. I've got goose bumps. I don't want to think about him. I'm breathing as if I were dying. There's not enough air and everything else is too much. A tear rolls from my eye, stings my sunburnt skin, and slides into my ear to rejoin the water inside me.

Phalange

One of the most painful things that's ever happened to me was the time I broke a phalange.

This was at home, not too long ago. I slipped and fell in the bathtub, and that phalange saved my life. I fell on my hand to protect my head, which would have smashed like an egg on the floor.

I got dressed one-handed, not bothering to dry off, and went outside in tears to hail a taxi. The cab driver saw my hand and understood. He took me straight to the hospital.

I had never had an X-ray before. The radiologist left me alone, machine clanking away. It was so loud and so ugly, and no one had told me what was going on, and I have no tolerance for pain, and it was all too much for me and I fainted.

I'd thought the radiologist had left the room because something bad was going to happen, and it did. I hit the X-ray table face first, right as the machine started to scan.

When the doctor saw the X-ray of my skull, he said I was fine. I'd cut my forehead, that's all. I held up my hand with the broken phalange and the doctor said, "Oh, right. That."

He took my hand in his like a veterinarian holding a dying bird. Then he called the nurse, who brought a cast.

It turns out that a cast is just a bandage. They dip it in water—I don't know if the water was hot, but it burned when it touched my skin—and then it turns into a cast. Before this, I thought giving someone a cast was practically sculpture.

The nurse wrapped up my whole finger and kept going. When she got past my wrist I said, "It was just the finger."

"I'm making a splint," she said, and so the cast went along the inside of my arm, with bandages holding it to the outside.

The doctor gave me Faldene for the pain and, when I stood up to go, said, "What about your head?"

My head didn't hurt. I barely hit it at all. It was like when a party ends and you drop your head on the table to show you're ready to go. But a person who goes to psychotherapy every month can't say to a doctor, "No, my head's fine."

So I let him bandage my head.

I went home with my bandaged head and my arm in a cast. "I had an accident," I said, and it was true.

For the next few days I kept the bandage on. I liked to watch how people reacted. Occasionally I rolled my eyes around and stuttered so that people would think there was something wrong with my head for real.

I walked around that way until it was time to get my cast off. I figured I'd have the doctor take the bandage off my head, too.

He sawed off the cast, then unwrapped the bandage and said, "I knew there was nothing wrong with your head. Look, the bandage is perfectly clean. You washed it, right? You must have. You tied it like a bandanna."

"I never said I hurt my head, but I've been walking around like this for fun. There's got to be something wrong with me."

"Or with me," the doctor said. He smiled, eyes wide and bright. I thought he was going to stab me with his scalpel or drug me. Instead he asked if I wanted to see the blood bank.

I said yes, and we went down to a basement that looked like the vaults in an actual bank. There were bags of blood everywhere. I touched them and it was like touching red blood cells.

The doctor said you can identify blood type by color and taste. I made him prove it. I filled test tubes with blood for him to try, but he just dipped his finger in the blood and touched it to his tongue. I had thought he'd drink it all. I wanted him to.

He identified all the blood correctly. O+ was the sweetest, and then the rest of the positives. The negatives tasted more like iron or salt, depending on the letter.

When I left, the doctor gave me a bit of my cast. I use it sometimes to pretend I've hurt my hand and can't write or hurt my foot and can't go someplace I never wanted to go to begin with.

I didn't accept the bag of blood he offered. That seemed like too much.

Blood Calls

I'm a nurse, so not much upsets me, and certainly I have no problem with blood. I work with blood, you could say. Blood for me is like oil for a cook. And so I wasn't worried on the morning I woke up with a long scab running down my left cheek.

I stood in front of the mirror and picked at the scab with my nails, which is something I enjoy as much as anyone else does. Unfortunately, it isn't permitted at work.

When the scab was gone, I washed my face and shaved gingerly, looking for a cut or scratch. I could have injured myself in the night, I thought. Once I left a knife on my nightstand and cut my finger when I tried to snooze my alarm the next morning. But I shaved my whole face and felt nothing. There had been no cut, just blood.

I figured I must have had a nosebleed. I get those

when I'm stressed. The day I took my final nursing exam, my nose bled all over the test. I wasn't embarrassed, though. The stains didn't bother me. I even let the blood drip on the desk to show the examiners how little I cared. See, I told them silently, I was born to be a nurse.

As I ate breakfast I thought about the scab. I dipped a finger in my orange juice and ran it down my face, waiting to feel a sting, but no luck. There was no cut. Nosebleed, for sure. It made sense. I'd had a stress dream that night, the one about two-headed horses. In the dream I own a stable. An army of hunters comes after my horses with poison gas, and I have to escape with my animals, each horse tossing its two heads.

At work I told Rosita what happened. By then I had stopped worrying about the scab, but I wanted her to worry, to touch my face with her long clean fingers, her perfectly manicured nails. She wasn't the brightest, Rosita, but she was a good person, cheerful, kind, and beautiful. When she was young, she wanted to be a doctor, but she couldn't handle the med school coursework and settled for being a lab nurse instead. But the work bored her, and she jumped at the chance to talk to anyone who told her they were in pain or felt sick. She even wrote prescriptions if you let her. In all honesty, it was a bit of an obsession. She had a prescription pad with her name in gold letters, and used it to write diet tips and recipes, leave people notes, give her number to male nurses she liked.

I was in love with Rosita, and I thought she might be interested in me. I was sure that when I told her about the scab, she'd want to take a look. She touched my cheek gently, bringing her face close to mine, squinting as she searched for a wound. Her perfume was like a dry wave. Her warm, minty breath touched my ears. I was sweaty and frightened. It was the best thing that had happened to me in weeks. Then my nose started to bleed.

Her first response was to put her hand under my nostrils to stop the blood. Then she remembered we were surrounded by bandages and cotton balls and laughed—she was even prettier when she laughed— and wiped her bloody hand on my cheeks, which turned me on even more, which of course made my nose bleed harder.

She made two gauze plugs for my nostrils, then dug a pack of towelettes from her purse and cleaned my face. "They're for removing makeup," she explained. "They're moisturizing, too, which is good, since your skin's a bit dry."

I was enchanted and mute. All I could do was smile, mouth open, since I couldn't breathe through my nose. Rosita took out her prescription pad with its gold-plated letters, as pretty as she was, as pretty as her name. *Vitamin K supplements*, she wrote, and *alfalfa and parsley with orange juice in the mornings*.

So that was the end of my workday: head spinning with happiness, gauze up my nose, Rosita's writing in my hand, her skin on my skin, her advice written down in my pocket.

I walked to the pharmacy, thinking about whether I should ask Rosita on a date. The pharmacist laughed when she saw my prescription. I was embarrassed, but only a little. Mostly I wanted to make Rosita happy, so the next morning I found her on break and told her I'd bought the supplements and was feeling healthier already. She seemed pleased, so I went on, "Rosita, I'm so sorry you couldn't afford medical school. You would have been such a good doctor. My nose stopped bleeding, my skin looks better—Rosita, do you want to go out with me?"

And she said yes. We got a drink, or a few drinks; went dancing; and finally, once we were drunk, wound up in her bed. I told her the nosebleed the day before had started because she turned me on so much, and then went back to praising her medical abilities, telling her I trusted her so much I'd begged some alfalfa from my neighbor who keeps rabbits after I'd failed to find it at the supermarket.

She didn't respond right away. When she did, she sounded annoyed. "So what, you got a nosebleed because I turn you on, but you're not bleeding now. Don't you like me? I want to see you bleed."

"But Rosita, you fixed it! You cured the nosebleed. You're the doctor I needed. Everyone else is missing out."

She rolled on top of me and we made love again.

After that I kept taking my vitamins and alfalfa, and my relationship with Rosita improved. We'd even joke about how my nosebleed got us together.

But then I woke up with a new scab. I'd had a good dream, one where Rosita and I were dancing in an empty ballroom. I couldn't tell her. She'd be upset if she knew my nosebleeds were back. It would mean her prescription had failed. All right, then. Even if I bled every day from now on, I'd clean the blood up myself.

I stayed in bed, picking at my scab and thinking about Rosita, until I was interrupted by a drop of blood on my face. It wasn't mine. I looked up and there was blood welling out of one of the nursing textbooks on the shelf above my bed.

It must be the heart attack chapter, I thought, or some other section about heart trouble, but when I opened the book, I saw that the blood came from a picture of my former girlfriend. This was the one who cheated on me, the least attractive woman I ever dated, the one I was with the longest and understood the least.

The photograph wouldn't stop bleeding. I found a specimen cup to collect the blood. I remembered that I'd meant to get rid of everything that reminded me of her, but that I'd left a few pictures in a box in the garage, and sure enough, when I checked the box was bleeding. There was at least a liter of blood. I collected some of it, then looked at the photos. They were all bleeding.

I brought the specimen to Rosita. I told her a friend of mine had found it in a cooler outside his door and wanted to do a lab analysis so he'd know where it came from. Rosita, who believes in witchcraft and voodoo, wouldn't touch it. She made me give it to one of her coworkers to test. She insisted on taking some of my blood, too, in case the evil from the other sample had fallen on me.

"There's no way this blood isn't cursed," she said. "My coworker says it's contaminated. You should tell your friend to be careful. But you don't have to worry, sweetie. Your blood's fine."

That day I called my ex to find out if she wept blood. She picked up the phone and burst into tears when I said it was me.

"Are you crying blood?" I asked.

She cried harder. "After all this time, you're calling to make fun of me?"

We only spoke for a moment. She said it was hard for her to hear my voice. Then she said she needed me; she wanted to see me. She begged me to come visit her.

I went that afternoon. She was clearly sick and upset. She'd lost weight and had dark bags under her eyes. Her house was a mess; her father had died; she was totally alone. She told me that the doctors didn't understand it, but her organs were turning to liquid one by one. Her body was coming apart from inside.

She asked me to stay with her. She thought she'd

get better if I was there. She needed a nurse. She didn't have to be my girlfriend, she said. Just my patient.

When I went home the photos had stopped bleeding. I called my ex-girlfriend right away. She answered the phone sounding better, more animated, and I said that I had decided to come take care of her. I'd quit my job, I told her, and I thought we should look for a smaller house to live in, a new house outside the city, someplace less polluted.

I don't know why I said all that, but I meant it. I didn't mention the photos. I remembered what Rosita said about spells and I wondered if somebody had cast one on me. But I know that in life, we get attached to things. They don't tie you down, but they get in your way, and the more you try to escape, the more they follow you. Ball and chain, my father used to say when he was drunk. My mother would say it too, while she scrubbed his vomit from the rugs in the morning. Ball and chain.

I wrote Rosita a letter, but I didn't explain much. I used the words *forces outside my control*. I told her that I was sorry, that I'd always love her, that it hurt me terribly to leave. Then I enclosed some pictures of myself and some more of me and Rosita together.

I still take vitamin K, and I grow alfalfa in my garden. She's doing better now that she follows Rosita's prescription; she's so much better that I rarely worry about the health of our first child, but last night I dreamed about two-headed horses. Rosita was there, riding with me. We were happy. It's been a long time since I left her, but I'm hoping this means somewhere, my picture has started to bleed.

Å Håpe

*

Norwegian has three words for waiting: å vente, å forvente, å håpe.

The first is waiting for buses; the second is waiting for other people; the third is waiting for something you want.

In English: *to wait, to expect, to hope.*

In Spanish, all we have is *esperar.* One word. It doesn't even tell you how long you're waiting.

Waiting

Like they say, waiting annoys people. It's true.

At the moment I'm waiting for January, because this December I fell apart.

For a few days I've been waiting for some stamps to arrive.

I waited for a delayed flight.

I waited for answers.

I waited in a bar for hours, and outside in the sun.

I waited for myself in a hotel room in Oslo.

I waited for sleep.

I turned every place I went into a waiting room, but I always felt exposed. I was irritated and raw. I was so sensitive you could have brushed me with a feather, and I would have howled.

If you wait long enough, you get bedsores. You're the same as a patient in a coma, lying on her back in bed, waiting for her mind to return.

A Trip

Recently I took a trip to my cat's stomach. It wasn't hard. First I took a long shower so my body could soak up water. Once my skin was leaking, I went out to the garden without getting dressed and curled up in the sunlight to dry. When it got dark, I moved inside to finish the process in front of the stove. It sucked the moisture out of me and sealed my pores shut. I turned into a piece of dried meat.

I knew I would have to wait a while for my cat to get hungry enough to eat me or bored enough to play with me. When he came over to investigate my body, the first thing he ate was my eyes, which had been very difficult to dry out. They were shriveled like raisins when the rest of me was as hard as jerky or salt cod or those pigs' ears they sell at the pet store.

My cat ate a bit more of me every day. He worked through my muscles to my intestines, which hadn't hardened completely and must have been a nice break for his jaws. Then he swallowed my skeleton, and inside his stomach I became whole.

All I saw in my cat's stomach was hair. Like all cats, he cleans himself constantly, and so more hairs appeared every day. They stuck to me until it looked like he'd eaten a Chewbacca toy. But eventually the hairs stopped coming, and I began to worry about my poor cat's health. No one was feeding him. It was time for me to go home.

I climbed up his throat, passing his lungs and heart, and stood on the place where he purrs. There, I stretched as tall as I could and managed to touch the back of his tongue. He hiccupped and puked me out.

The hairs stuck to my skin softened the landing. Still, it took a few days until I was ready to crawl to the bathroom. When I got there, I was too small to turn the shower on. Instead I jumped into the toilet tank and stayed there, like a fetus in a ceramic womb, moving my arms and legs and soaking up the bacteria my immune system needed. Once I had grown larger than the drain, I flushed the toilet to suck the remaining hairs away.

Now I'm naked and getting bigger. I'm still not ready to go to work, but I still have a few more vacation days left. Yes, I took my vacation inside my cat's stomach. These days I'm frightened of airports. And besides, it's always safer to travel with someone you know.

Acknowledgments

Some of these stories have appeared previously in the following publications:

Tin House: "A Trip"
Contra Viento: "Fish" and "Plasticine Dreams"
Latin American Literature Today: "Eloísa" and
    "Swimming Pool"
Electric Lit: "Little Bird"
MAKE: "A Writer's Pastimes"

Enormous thanks to: Will Evans, Jill Meyers, and everyone at Deep Vellum; Andrea Palet at Libros del Laurel, who introduced us; the editors whose literary magazines first published stories from *Little Bird* in English; and our agents, Víctor Hurtado and Sarah Burnes. And eternal thanks to Claudia, for trusting me with your work.

—Lily

About the Author

Claudia Ulloa Donoso is the author of *El pez que aprendió a caminar*, *Séptima madrugada*, and *Pajarito*, which has been published in six countries and translated into English and French. In 2017, the Hay Festival named her to the Bogotá 39 list of the most outstanding Latin American writers working today. Claudia was born in Lima and lives in Bodø, Norway, where she teaches Spanish and Norwegian to immigrants.

About the Translator

Lily Meyer is a writer, translator, and critic from Washington, D.C. Her story translations have appeared in *The Brooklyn Rail*, *Contra Viento*, *Electric Literature*, *Joyland*, *Latin American Literature Today*, *MAKE*, and *Tin House*. She is a PhD candidate in fiction at the University of Cincinnati. *Little Bird* is her first full-length translation.

PARTNERS

pixel ||| texel

EMBREY FAMILY
FOUNDATION

ALLRED
CAPITAL MANAGEMENT
RAYMOND JAMES®

ADDITIONAL DONORS, CONT'D

Mark Haber
Mary Cline
Maynard Thomson
Michael Reklis
Mike Soto
Mokhtar Ramadan
Nikki & Dennis Gibson
Patrick Kukucka
Patrick Kutcher
Rev. Elizabeth & Neil Moseley
Richard Meyer

Scott & Katy Nimmons
Sherry Perry
Sydneyann Binion
Stephen Harding
Stephen Williamson
Susan Carp
Susan Ernst
Theater Jones
Tim Perttula
Tony Thomson

SUBSCRIBERS

Ned Russin
Michael Binkley
Michael Schneiderman
Aviya Kushner
Kenneth McClain
Eugenie Cha
Stephen Fuller
Joseph Rebella
Brian Matthew Kim
Anthony Brown

Michael Lighty
Ryan Todd
Erin Kubatzky
Shelby Vincent
Margaret Terwey
Ben Fountain
Caitlin Jans
Gina Rios
Alex Harris

AVAILABLE NOW FROM DEEP VELLUM

MICHÈLE AUDIN · *One Hundred Twenty-One Days*
translated by Christiana Hills · FRANCE

BAE SUAH · *Recitation*
translated by Deborah Smith · SOUTH KOREA

MARIO BELLATIN · *Mrs. Murakami's Garden*
translated by Heather Cleary · MEXICO

EDUARDO BERTI · *The Imagined Land*
translated by Charlotte Coombe · ARGENTINA

CARMEN BOULLOSA · *Texas: The Great Theft* · *Before* · *Heavens on Earth*
translated by Samantha Schnee · Peter Bush · Shelby Vincent · MEXICO

MAGDA CARNECI · *FEM*
translated by Sean Cotter · ROMANIA

LEILA S. CHUDORI · *Home*
translated by John H. McGlynn · INDONESIA

SARAH CLEAVE, ed. · *Banthology: Stories from Banned Nations* ·
IRAN, IRAQ, LIBYA, SOMALIA, SUDAN, SYRIA & YEMEN

ANANDA DEVI · *Eve Out of Her Ruins*
translated by Jeffrey Zuckerman · MAURITIUS

PETER DIMOCK · *Daybook from Sheep Meadow* · USA

ROSS FARRAR · *Ross Sings Cheree & the Animated Dark: Poems* · USA

ALISA GANIEVA · *Bride and Groom* · *The Mountain and the Wall*
translated by Carol Apollonio · RUSSIA

ANNE GARRÉTA · *Sphinx* · *Not One Day*
translated by Emma Ramadan · FRANCE

JÓN GNARR · *The Indian* · *The Pirate* · *The Outlaw*
translated by Lytton Smith · ICELAND

GOETHE · *The Golden Goblet: Selected Poems* · *Faust, Part One*
translated by Zsuzsanna Ozsváth and Frederick Turner · GERMANY

NOEMI JAFFE · *What are the Blind Men Dreaming?*
translated by Julia Sanches & Ellen Elias-Bursac · BRAZIL

CLAUDIA SALAZAR JIMÉNEZ · *Blood of the Dawn*
translated by Elizabeth Bryer · PERU

JUNG YOUNG MOON · *Seven Samurai Swept Away in a River* · *Vaseline Buddha*
translated by Yewon Jung · SOUTH KOREA

KIM YIDEUM · *Blood Sisters*
translated by Ji yoon Lee · SOUTH KOREA

JOSEFINE KLOUGART · *Of Darkness*
translated by Martin Aitken · DENMARK

YANICK LAHENS · *Moonbath*
translated by Emily Gogolak · HAITI

FORTHCOMING FROM DEEP VELLUM

MIRCEA CĂRTĂRESCU · *Solenoid*
translated by Sean Cotter · ROMANIA

MATHILDE CLARK · *Lone Star*
translated by Martin Aitken · DENMARK

LOGEN CURE · *Welcome to Midland: Poems* · USA

CLAUDIA ULLOA DONOSO · *Little Bird*, translated by Lily Meyer · PERU/NORWAY

LEYLÂ ERBIL · *A Strange Woman*
translated by Nermin Menemencioğlu · TURKEY

FERNANDA GARCIA LAU · *Out of the Cage*
translated by Will Vanderhyden · ARGENTINA

ANNE GARRÉTA · *In/concrete*
translated by Emma Ramadan · FRANCE

JUNG YOUNG MOON · *Arriving in a Thick Fog*
translated by Mah Eunji and Jeffrey Karvonen · SOUTH KOREA

FISTON MWANZA MUJILA · *The Villain's Dance*, translated by Roland Glasser · *The River in the Belly: Selected Poems*, translated by Bret Maney · DEMOCRATIC REPUBLIC OF CONGO

LUDMILLA PETRUSHEVSKAYA · *Kidnapped: A Crime Story*, translated by Marian Schwartz · *The New Adventures of Helen: Magical Tales*, translated by Jane Bugaeva · RUSSIA

JULIE POOLE · *Bright Specimen: Poems from the Texas Herbarium* · USA

MANON STEFAN ROS · *The Blue Book of Nebo* · WALES

ETHAN RUTHERFORD · *Farthest South & Other Stories* · USA

BOB TRAMMELL · *The Origins of the Avant-Garde in Dallas & Other Stories* · USA